Life in the Alaskan Wild

Moving Forward

An Alaskan Adventure Novel

By Charles Kalmon
Illustrations by Jenny Newell

Book #2

# Chapter 1
## The Addition

We needed more supplies for the cabin addition than we had originally realized. Because of this, we had to make another trip to Fairbanks, and that cost us time, which was in limited supply, to get everything transported upriver to our cabin home. As far as money was concerned, it meant nothing to us because we knew that we were building out future in the Alaskan wild. All of the extras were well worth it because soon our home would be completed. As always, time flies by, and this year was no different. As we worked long days, we were constantly in wonder at how fast the day turned to night. It was June, and the days were long, almost twenty hours of daylight.

The long days now were wonderful, but things change, and winter comes early this far north in Alaska. That meant the cabin addition had to be finished before the first snow flew or it would complicate the entire building process. And, to make matters worse, the scouting work for the trapping season would potentially be set back as a result. Our agenda was set. The first order of business that kept Jen and me busy for a couple of days was figuring out exactly how to proceed with the cabin foundation.

We decided to build the addition on pylons, keeping the floor a couple of feet off the ground. Then, to prevent the wind from blowing under our floor boards, we would frame the sidewalls all the way to the ground and run the siding boards to the ground or a little bit below the surface. We figured that this building technique would help us keep the cabin warm. Also, we planned to run six inches of batting insulation between the underneath set of floor boards and the flooring on the inside of the cabin. This would hold in heat which would be produced by a second wood stove that would be set up in the addition.

We started the building process by measuring to four corners of the addition, and then marking the spots by digging out an inch or two of soil from the places where we planned to put in the pylons. This worked quite well, but it took us several trips back and forth to get everything as close to square as possible. In the end, we decided that the addition was not perfectly square, but was square enough for us. We laughed at our process as we took a break in the beautiful summer air and the warm sunshine.

By the end of the day we had all of the pylons dug in and set. To prevent frost heaving, I dug them down to a depth that was over six feet. My posthole digger handles were not long enough to reach that far, so I duct taped some sturdy alder sticks to them to extend their length. This worked because I did not need the handles to be super strong, just needed them to allow me to clamp onto the loose dirt at the bottom of the hole. It worked out. After each green treated pylon was set, there was still three to four feet remaining above ground. I would have to cut them down eventually, but first wanted to nail on my floor frame to make sure everything was level. When that was achieved, I would saw off the extra lengths and save those pieces for another project. That work was for another day. *Probably tomorrow*, I thought.

I had spent most of the afternoon working by myself and at one point realized that I had not seen Jen for quite some time. I looked around and called her name.

"Right here." She said. "By the fire pit."

"Oh," I said. "You mean the fire pit right in front of me?"

"Yes, you silly man."

Jen had food ready and was waiting patiently by the fire. She had unfolded a couple of camp chairs and placed our supper on a makeshift table which I had constructed during my first year. I did not see her because she was stretched out in one of the chairs reading a book. I joined her and then dove into the sandwich she had waiting for me. After a few bites and some thought, it occurred to me that I had not seen Pretty Girl all day. I asked Jen if she had seen her lurking around in hopes of getting a sandwich for herself.

"No, I have not seen her." Jen said.

"Hmm." I grunted. "I wonder what she is up to."

"You never know," Jen responded, still reading her book.

"Well, I suppose, she is a wild bear, and, maybe has decided to move on. Keeping her for a pet is probably not a reality," I replied with a little sadness in my voice. "Yet, I have become very attached to her, and under the circumstances of how we came together, I feel like her mother, her protector."

"Okay, momma bear, go find your baby," she teased.

"Jen", I whined. "You know what I mean."

"I do, just teasing you. Let's eat our lunch and go look for her."

"Sounds good," I replied. "We will probably find her sleeping down by the river or up in her hillside den. She likes to crawl in there for a nap once in a while."

4

After supper Jen and I walked down to the river and then up river past our cabin. Pretty Girl was nowhere to be seen. As we walked back to the cabin, I realized that I had neglected to bring my rifle along for protection. Before we went up the hill to Pretty Girl's den site, I grabbed the always loaded 30-06 and threw it across my shoulder. When we got about halfway up the hill, we could see that Pretty Girl was not in her den, and by the looks of things had not napped there for a day or two. Because of how busy we were with the building of the addition, I didn't have much time to spend with my little bear. I figured that it was about time for me to come to terms with her returning to the wild. As I thought about that more, it became somewhat okay with me; I realized that was how her life was meant to be. Understanding this, on another level, however, did not make the actual idea of letting her go any easier to think about.

Back at the cabin, Jen and I decided to take advantage of the summer daylight and immediately began measuring and nailing in place our floor joist hangers. These little pre-shaped devices worked great. Once nailed in place, we simply had to cut the joists to length, drop them gently into the hangers on each end, and then tack them in place with nails. In no time at all we had the joists securely set in place. By dark we had both the upper and lower floors nailed in place encasing the insulation in the floor. Just as I had figured, this produced an incredibly stable foundation. Our addition was beginning to look like a part of our home. *Tomorrow,* I thought, *I will start on the walls and get them up and set in place.*

Jen went inside about an hour before me, and when I entered the cabin I was thankful that she had gone inside. It smelled like a bakery. Fresh baked bread scented the air, and mixed in, for sure, was the smell of moose stew. That assumption was correct; while I was outside, Jen opened a jar of moose meat and combined it with some of our stored onions, carrots, and potatoes. She was a genius in the kitchen.

"Who taught you to cook?" I asked.

"My Aunt Alice," she replied, with an ear to ear smile gracing her face.

"Thank you, Aunt Alice," I said as I gave my beautiful wife a peck on the cheek.

"Based on all the hammer pounding I heard, you must have achieved a lot out there after I left."

"Yes, I did. I got on a roll and had a hard time putting the hammer down. I am ready to do the walls tomorrow, and with any luck, get the floor joists for the upstairs hung, and maybe the upstairs flooring down too."

"Wow," Jen said, that would be great if you got all of that done. What would come after that?"

"The roof, and I am not looking forward to that work. We have prefabricated trusses, but they are hard to lift and put in place because of their bulkiness."

"Then you will need my help," Jen offered.

"Yes", I said, "most definitely."

The conversation died, and we ate quietly that night, mainly because it was late and we were tired. For me it was a little more than being tired. Even though I knew Pretty Girl and I would have to part ways eventually, my worries for her continued. I just could not get her out of my mind. She was small for her age, and had grown accustomed to being around me. Therefore, because she does not fear humans, she might fall prey to bear hunters. My hope was that no reasonable hunter out there would shoot a bear that small. Another worry I had was that other bears and probably wolves might see her as an easy meal. All I could do was hope for the best, and keep my eyes peeled for her. Before I knew it, my food was gone and I was staring at an empty plate. Jen woke me from my trance. "Did you enjoy your supper?"

"Supper was delicious. If at all possible," I said back to her, "this meal tasted better than it smelled."

"Thank you for making this fine meal. It is a favorite of mine."

"You are welcome, sweetheart," she said with a sly grin on her face.

That was the same phrase Aunt Alice used when talking to Alvin. I liked that about Jen. She picked up a lot of great things from her Auntie.

"Do you want to get started early in the morning, or is there another job that needs doing first?" I asked.

"I have no other immediate plans, but we do have to start on firewood pretty soon." Jen replied.

"That is for sure." I said. "After the roof is on and shingled, I will feel much better about the building project and then can focus on other things like firewood."

We finished our discussion while doing the dishes and then went to bed. It was midnight. I woke up the next morning and quietly made coffee and then headed outside to build a fire and sit by it and sip my morning coffee until I felt fully awake. My quiet time would also give Jen more time to catch some Z's.

After two cups, I had to get moving. The itch to complete the roof and shingles was pestering me. I started the day by building the eight-foot side walls. I did this by laying out all of the materials on the addition floor, where I then measured and cut all of the lumber needed. I spaced the wall studs sixteen inches on center and nailed them together. While the wall section was still on the floor, I framed in the window openings. This would make the work of putting windows in much easier once the walls were standing in place. The first wall was done in less than an hour and a half, so I hefted it up by myself and balanced it in place, perfectly matching the edge of the floor on that side. Keeping the wall balanced with one hand, while nailing a support piece in place with the other hand, created a precarious moment or two, but I got it done. I was feeling rather proud of myself and felt that a break was in order. With my empty coffee cup in hand I headed around the cabin to the front door where Jen was coming out. We saw each other just in time to avoid a collision in which the hot coffee and buttered toast she was carrying would have lost their lives.

"Well, good morning sunshine," Jen said with that ever-present smile spread across her face.

"Good morning, Babe! How did you sleep?"

"Great until some crazy carpenter started building a house next door."

"Ha-ha," I laughed. "I got the bug to build and just could not hold it back."

"That's good. I just laid back in bed and enjoyed the sounds of you building our future. It was very pleasing to listen to."

"It is a great morning," I said. "Warm and not much wind. Let's go around back and I will show you what I have done."

We walked around the cabin to the addition. I could immediately see that Jen was pleased.

"You raised that wall by yourself?"

"Yes, I did. It is not very heavy, but there were a few moments where I thought it might tip over on me. Don't lean on it because it is only tacked in place."

"I won't. Do you want to sit out here and have some toast and more coffee?"

"Yes! I am starving."

Jen poured coffee in my cup and handed me two thickly sliced pieces of toast. As we talked and ate our breakfast, we decided, as we looked things over, that we were very happy with our decision to buy extra windows. Our bedroom upstairs would have two, three foot by four-foot windows on each wall. That would give us incredible light both at night and during the day. What we liked most about it was that we would have the feeling that we were sleeping outside. This was very important to both of us.

This far out in the wilds of Alaska, there are no other lights to interfere with the light from the moon and stars. It gives a surreal sense to a person awakening in the night. I hoped to have those six windows in by the end of the week. There would be two small windows on the side of the addition that butted up to original cabin, for a total of eight windows upstairs. The two small ones would allow us to see out and over the roof because the old cabin was only one story high.

We were lost in our conversation when the crunch of a snapped twig behind us caught our attention. I whirled around thinking that a big old bear had caught scent of our breakfast and was sneaking in for a sample. I was relieved to see it was Pretty Girl.

"Hey, Pretty Girl," I said with delight. "Where the heck have you been?" I asked half expecting an answer. She lumbered around the addition paying very little attention to the changes to our home. She sat on her haunches facing us about five feet away and sniffed the air while grunting her gentle little tough-girl grunts. We laughed.

"Does she do that because she is trying to remember exactly who we are?" Jen asked.

"I think so," I said. "It seems that the basic recognition is always there, but she has to go through her naturally given senses to assure herself that all is good. I guess you could say it is a confirmation process."

"That makes sense. Should I give her some toast?"

"Sure," I said. "She is probably waiting for breakfast."

Jen held out a piece of toast. Pretty Girl immediately raised to her feet and sauntered gently over to accept the buttered gift.

"Do we have anything left from yesterday that we can share with her?" I asked.

"We do," Jen said. "I have been saving bread and other scraps of food in hopes that she would return. I will go get it."

"Come on Pretty Girl," Jen coaxingly called as she headed to the cabin door. Pretty Girl dutifully followed because she knew what was in store for her. Finally, Pretty Girl had made an appearance. I was so happy to have her back. My worries went to the wayside. I hoped she would never again disappear.

With a big smile on my face, I went back to work building the other two walls and then attaching the walls of the addition to the walls of the main cabin. The days flew by, and by the middle of June we had the roof on and completely shingled, had all the windows in, and all of the insulation in the new walls. Finally, it was time to cut out a section of the wall in the original cabin so that we could connect the two structures, making them one, and then get everything settled in the new addition.

Jen was excited to finally be able to utilize the new space created by the two-story addition. The next morning, we woke early, and because of our excitement bypassed our coffee and breakfast, going directly to work on cutting out the wall. I had this job figured out well before hand. I would use my chainsaw to do all the cutting. Before I began, Jen ran upstairs in the addition and opened all the windows while I opened the downstairs windows and the door. This would create a draft so the power saw exhaust fumes could escape the cabin. It was a cool, breezy morning-a great day to finalize this portion of the project.

When we had everything set, I fired up the chainsaw and followed my predetermined, chalk-marked line that when cut all the way around would reveal an eight-foot-wide entrance between the cabin and the addition. I had pulled all of the nails out of the wall before the saw work began. Because of this, and a little bit of luck, I did not hit any nails. They would have been very destructive to the chain. When this was done, Jen and I lowered the cut-out section of wall down so that the top of it rested on two homemade sawhorses. They supported the wall section and allowed me to saw it in half. After the final cut was made, I shut off the saw for the final time, and between the two of us dragged the sections outside by the fire pit.

We walked back in the cabin together and admired all the work we had completed. It seemed strange to us to have so much room. The stairs up to our bedroom were against the back wall of the addition. Under the stairs would be a great storage area, but that would have to wait. We had a lot of cleanup work to do, and there was no better time than now to get it done. While Jen managed the broom and dustpan, I spent time putting the tools away and then carrying the materials for our new bed upstairs.

By the time we were ready to make breakfast it was 7:30 in the morning, and had been over three hours since the sun came up. We really enjoyed these long days. Even though we were extremely tired at night, so much had been accomplished and that made us feel like we were gradually getting everything set for winter, which was the ultimate goal.

While we were making pancakes for breakfast on the propane stove, Pretty Girl wandered in and took up her favorite spot next to the wood stove. There was no fire in that stove, so she was not there for the heat. No, she was there watching Jen prepare breakfast and to remind us that she was a part of this family, and expected a plate of food be served to her. She was fun to watch. She laid there just like a puppy waiting for her food. Her patience was rewarded. She received a plate heaped with cakes topped with blueberries and sugar. Pretty Girl wasted no time in devouring her food. Sometimes I wondered if she had time to taste what she was eating. For the most part Pretty Girl's eating pattern was gulp, gulp, gone. Jen and I took our time. Eventually my little bear grew impatient with our slow eating style and went outside, probably to take a nap in the sunshine.

After a sip of coffee and a few more bites of my food I asked Jen if she was excited to spend our first night in our new upstairs bedroom. "I am," she said.

"Well then," I said. "I better get the bed frame built so we can put that new mattress down and put it to good use."

"Yes," replied Jen. "It is going to feel so good after spending all this time sleeping on your bunk that was built for one."

"Ha-ha, yes. It was a bit crowded."

"Since we have so much room now, we should move that bunk under the stairs for company to sleep on," Jen said. "Remember, Aunt Alice will be here for a visit soon."

"Yes, that is the perfect spot because we can store things underneath the bunk. It will serve double duty."

"And," Jen added, "We can curtain that area off to give Auntie some privacy during her visit."

"Then it is all figured out," I said. "I will get to work on that immediately."

"Okay, I will clean up the kitchen and then come help you."

"Excellent, I will move the bunk first and give you some options for what we can do with the extra space that it leaves in the kitchen."

With that, we were off building and organizing our cabin home. The cot was easy to move in one piece. I had not nailed it to the wall or to the floor, so my only task was to drag it across the floor to its resting spot under the stairs. I put the foot end under the lower end of the stairs so that anyone sleeping there would not bang a head on the stairs. The pillow end of the bunk faced the higher end and would give the guest plenty of head room.

I was happy with that job so I bounded up the stairs and measured the lumber to build the frame for our full-sized mattress. The work went well. I found that all the thinking and work I had put in to building the addition was coming in handy for all the other carpentry chores that presented themselves. After the cabin was completed, I reminded myself, the woodshed would be the next major building project. For now, the cabin had my full attention. In a matter of hours, and with Jen's help, we had the bed frame built. Most of Jen's extra time was spent carrying things upstairs, and now she was actively putting items where she wanted them. I am not much of a decorator so left her to the fun she was having.

I went outside for some fresh air. It was a beautiful day. Even though it was five-thirty in the evening, it would be light for many hours yet. I looked around for things that I could do but lost interest in doing any work. Then I noticed my fishing rods leaning against the cabin. I darted inside the cabin and yelled to Jen, "Let's go fishing."

She hollered back, "Give me a minute and I will be right down."

"Okay. I will be outside."

I went out the door and gathered the net and two fishing rods and tied baits on both of them. I was excited because fishing had been on my mind for some time, but the cabin was the priority for the last few weeks. Just as Jen was coming out the door, I was headed back in to get my rifle.

"Ready?" she asked.

"Yes I am."

I threw the rifle on my shoulder and grabbed the fishing equipment. Jen followed behind me and I could hear Pretty Girl behind her, grunting as she followed us down the trail.

The river was relatively low for this time of year. After all, the month of June is spring this far north. The snowpack had melted quickly, resulting in a quick rise of the water and then a fast lowering. The river was beautiful. I knew the fish would be biting.

Jen's fishing skills were better than mine. She had grown up at her Uncle Alvin's fish camp and had spent a great deal of time on the river banks. She had her first cast retrieved before I found a spot to fish.

"Come on slowpoke," she teased. "If you want fish for breakfast, we need to catch some."

"Ha-ha," I said, as my line sailed through the air and landed in her casting area.

"That is cheating. You can't fish in my place," she playfully snarled.

"I was just checking to be sure you didn't leave one in there after that first cast."

I did not catch one on that cast, but did want fresh fish for breakfast, so I got serious about fishing. We had each taken about ten casts before the first strike occurred. It was Jen who screamed with excitement.

"Got one!"

"Woot, woot! I hollered as I dropped my pole and ran for the net. It looked like a nice fish. It stayed deep for a while and then broke the surface several times, leaving huge swirls after splashing water in all directions.

"Check your drag," I warned. "I forgot to set it before we started casting."

"I set it," Jen said, as she concentrated on her fight with what we now knew was a giant pike.

"That is a huge fish, Jen, bigger than the ones I caught last year."

"I think it is about four feet," Jen said, "and I think it is going to take another run."

The fish did take another run, but it was straight toward her. Jen's line went limp and she momentarily thought she had lost the monster fish. From my angle I could see that he was cruising straight at her.

"Reel," I screamed in excitement. "Reel! He is coming toward you."

Jen had heard me, but did not say a word because she was frantically reeling up all the slack line. When the fish finally felt tension again, it realized it was not free and took line off the spool so fast that it seemed the friction would melt the whole fishing rig. We had a fight on our hands and knew this was not going to be an easy catch. The giant pike was back in deep water where he held the advantage, and, to make matters worse, Jen was getting tired. I could see this because she kept looking at me as if to say, you can take over anytime.

"Are you tired?" I asked.

"Yes," she replied, and then immediately, "but I want to catch him by myself." I saw a flash of determination in her eyes, and said, "You got it. I will get the net ready." Then, as an afterthought, "I hope that big fish will fit in the net."

After about five minutes more of back and forth runs and gains, Jen had the fish close enough to shore for me to attempt to net it. At this close range, I could finally see that the pike was definitely not going to fit in my less than impressive net. I could also see that the huge fish was lip hooked and that the back and forth battle had loosened the hook's grip and was at risk of falling out if any slack was allowed in the line.

"Keep the line tight, Jen, and I will wade out and get behind the fish. When I get in place, I will scoop him up and all in one motion toss it on shore."

"Okay," Jen agreed. "Don't let him get away."

I quietly moved out, trying my best to not create waves that might startle the fish, and was soon behind the behemoth, finned creature. The only problem was that he was facing the shore and that made it near impossible for me to shovel him to dry land. It would work best if it was broadside to the shore.

"Jen," I whispered, thinking that if I spoke loudly, the fish would start his fight again, "He is very tired. Move your rod tip to your right and try to gently force him to turn broadside."

"Okay," she whispered back without looking at me or moving her lips. Her focus and seriousness made me laugh so that my body shook, creating small ripples in the water, still I maintained my concentration. Jen's prodding of the fish worked. The big pike was exhausted and did not resist the movement. As soon as it was parallel to the shore I quietly placed my hands beneath the big brute's belly, and then with one great force slammed my hands and arms upward, launching it several feet up on the rocks of the shore.

Jen screamed with delight. "I got it, I got it! He is huge."

I ran to her side, then dropped to my knees and held the flopping fish down so it could not make its way back into the water.

"Nice job, Jen," I said, as I placed a congratulatory kiss on her cheek.

"Good work getting him to the shore. Net or no net, that was impressive!"

"Wow," she went on to say as her eyes admiringly scanned over the fish. "We have a lot of food here. I think our fishing is done until we get this one eaten up."

"He has to be close to sixty inches, we will probably have to can some of this." I said. "Pretty Girl will have a feast of the skin and innards."

That thought brought my attention to Pretty Girl. I looked around for my little bear and saw her casually watching us from a spot about twenty yards downstream. She did not seem overly impressed with our fishing skills, but after we collected the fishing tackle and headed toward the cabin, she was hot on our heels. She knew treats were in her near future.

Back at the cabin I began filleting the fish while Jen went inside to get a fry pan ready. We had decided to have a late-night supper of fish sandwiches. That went a long way to encourage me to rapidly clean the fish. By the time I was to the cabin door with the two massive fillets, Pretty Girl was done chewing up the fish remains. She looked content. I looked at her and said, "Are you coming in for a sandwich?" She just sat there and looked at me. My heart sank a little bit because I knew our days as friends were limited. It is the way of the wild. At least, I figured, she would be able to fend for herself if she walked away now. With a happy sadness in my heart, I went inside the cabin and closed the door.

I sat down at the table and with my pliers in hand began pulling the "Y" bones out of the fish fillets. When I had one slab done, I cut it into fry pan sizes and delivered them to Jen. She rinsed them and rolled the perfectly white chunks of pike in seasoned flour. I smiled with satisfaction as I heard them sizzle in the fry pan. By the time my work was done and the mess cleaned up, Jen had two big sandwiches waiting. They were delicious. Not much in the world beats the taste of fresh-fried fish.

It had been a long day. We were tired and ready to try out our new bedroom. We climbed the stairs by lantern light. Luckily, I had purchased several gas lanterns so the one I carried would be the permanent light in our bedroom. I hadn't thought about the need for light upstairs, so there was no place to hang it. But, because Jen had everything upstairs and neatly situated, there were some crates that could serve as night stands, and one worked great for a place to set our lantern. Jen had that all figured out.

In no time at all we were in bed and enjoying the spectacular night sights out our naturally lit room. With the lantern snuffed out for the night, all of the natural and wild light shone in. It was beautiful. As we talked about our day and what needed to be done, I noticed a huge cloud bank far off to the west, which no doubt, would soon engulf us. There would be heavy rain in those clouds. I hoped our work on the cabin was well done and there would be no leaks. With Jen in my arms and a smile on my face, we drifted from conversation to sleep.

## Chapter 2
## Early Morning Disaster

The sound seemed so unnatural. At first it was a low hum that quickly turned into a loud whine. "It's an airplane," I said to myself as I bolted up and out of bed. I had woken up a couple times during the night because of the noise the heavy rain was making as it pounded the roof. This was not the same sound. It was very different. I glanced at the clock that Jen had placed on a box in front of the bed. It was nine thirty in the morning, although it seemed much earlier because of the heavy, low-lying clouds that surrounded us.

The sound grew louder. I trotted to the window on the far side of our bedroom in time to see a transport prop plane fly by extremely low to the ground. In the heavy clouds, I could make out that there was smoke and flames coming from two of the engines and from the fuselage. I knew instantly that the plane was going to crash. Everything seemed to be in slow motion, and for a second, I could see the pilot's silhouette, ever so faintly. Although I could not see movement from him, he must have been frantically working to keep the plane from hitting the ground. His attempts were futile. In just a matter of seconds the plane was out of sight and moments later I heard a loud explosion that shook the windows and jolted Jen out of her

deep sleep

"What was that?" she screamed in terror.

"A plane crashed. It must be a little way over the hill that runs along the river. I saw it go down."

"What do you mean, a plane crashed?"

"It did," I said. "A transport plane, a big one. It flew right past the cabin and then disappeared and crashed."

"Oh gosh. No. That is horrible" Jen said, her voice shaking. "We have to go see if there are any survivors."

I was already bounding down the stairs. I laced up my boots and grabbed both of our rain jackets. With Jen on my heels we ran out of the cabin. We were unsure of what to do or take with us. As a last-minute thought, I went back in the cabin and strapped my pistol on and threw the 30-06 rifle over my shoulder. Back outside I found Jen.

She had an axe and was in the process of pouring gas in the chainsaw tank. As soon as she was done we ran down the trail to the river and turned upstream heading straight toward a giant stream of billowing black smoke. Fear tightened its grip in my chest. Nothing about this scene was going to be good.

*This is too much for anyone to survive*, I thought as we ran toward the crash site. Thinking that the only person onboard was the pilot, I whispered to myself, "I hope he is alive." Then the thought came to my mind that there surely had to be several people onboard. If this were a fact, the scene awaiting us would be one of unfathomable destruction.

As we got closer and climbed up the bank we could fully see the wreckage created by the crash. Because the flames were so intense, we figured they must have been carrying gas to a village and because of items that were strewn about, knew that they were delivering many other things that a remote village would need. After surveying the wreckage, a bit longer, we realized that the fuselage broke in half right behind the wings. It looked like someone sawed it in half. The back half of the plane was about two hundred yards from the front, and was not on fire. That is probably why we did not notice it right away. The front half of the plane was fully engulfed in flames. I turned to Jen. She was crying.

"There is no way anyone survived this crash," she said through her sobs.

"That is probably so, but we have to check."

"I am going to holler and see if anyone answers," I said.

"Okay."

I yelled at the top of my lungs. Nothing. We waited a moment hoping to hear cries for help, but they did not come. I yelled again. Nothing. Things did not look good.

I said to Jen,

"Let's go to the back part of the aircraft and see if anyone is there."

"Okay." She agreed.

I took her hand and then put my arm around Jen's shoulder and asked her if she wanted to wait by the river until I checked everything out.

"No," she said. "I want to be here if anyone needs help."

We pushed our way through the brush, and as we reached the back end of the plane could see that it was full of items that were meant for someone's home. We could see everything from a 4-wheeler that had been tossed from the plane, to chairs and tables, still all boxed up and strapped in. The contents of this part of the plane shifted some on impact, but were remarkably undamaged.

Still hoping that were survivors, I called out again and again. Jen joined in too, but we received no response. I climbed up and went into the tail section looking for people. There was no one to be seen. As I turned back to Jen, I shook my head and said, "They have all probably burned up."

"Oh, I hope not," she said. "That would be so tragic."

"Yes, it would be, but we have to be realistic."

"I know, but let's keep looking." Jen said as tears began streaming down her face again.

"That we will do. I bet there will be a rescue crew on the way very soon. It will probably be a chopper."

The fire was subsiding around the front part of the aircraft. Still, we could not get really close because the heat was incredibly intense, but did get close enough to see the remains of the pilot and the co-pilot still strapped in their seats. It was a grizzly sight. They were only recognizable by the human form that somewhat remained, appearing to be a smoldering skeleton. All else had been burned away. Jen began to cry harder, and I shed a few tears while holding her close and trying to decide what we should do. I wished a helicopter full of rescue workers would show up and deliver us from the task that had to be done. Now we knew that at least two people were killed, but still needed to find out if there were more crew members on board, who, hopefully, survived.

Unfortunately, the rain picked up and the wind switched to the north and, surprisingly, the temperature dropped quickly. I knew that this change in weather would likely hold back any rescue attempts even if they had missed the plane at this point. This meant that Jen and I were the search and rescue team for now. I looked around for a vantage point, and, finding one, decided to run up to its high point just to the front of the aircraft. This would give me a good view of the surrounding area. Jen found a place to sit while I climbed to the higher elevation. The view was good, but there was nothing to see but parts of the wreckage and miles of uninhabited land.

Dejection hit me hard while I was up there scanning the surroundings. I wished for a radio, a boat, or anything that would allow me to contact a rescue team. As I worked myself down the incline, searching the ground as I went, some movement far out in front of the burning aircraft caught my attention. It was a piece of clothing snagged on an alder branch, blowing in the stiff, cold wind. Something, however, did not seem right. Its motion was different from wind motion. I looked at it for a moment and when my focus was clear, realized it was a person lying on the ground with one arm in the air weakly waving back and forth, a signal for help.

"Jen," I yelled! "Over there!" I pointed in the direction of the movement and took off running at full speed.

Jen saw where I was going and raced in the same direction. When we got there, we found a young man staring weakly up at us and in a hoarse whisper he said,

"Help me, please help me."

"We are here," Jen whispered as she knelt down near his head. "You are safe now."

"Where do you hurt?"

"Everywhere! My legs, my legs mostly! They hurt so bad."

"Anywhere else with intense pain?" Jen asked, all the while searching him for external injuries.

"No," he said. "My legs are the worst of the pain."

"Does anything in your belly or chest hurt?"

"No, just my legs. I think they are both broken."

"Okay. Can you tell me how many people were on the plane?"

"Yes, three of us," he said through chattering teeth. "Are they okay?"

"No," Jen said. "I cannot lie to you. They did not make it. Were you guys friends?"

"Oh no. They are dead? No! We just met. This was my first flight with them. They were nice guys. Oh no, this is horrible. Tell me this is not really happening."

"I am sorry. It is true. What is your name?" I asked, trying to change the direction of the conversation.

"Kyle."

"Okay, Kyle, we need to get you back to our cabin. You are shivering and will get hypothermia if we do not get you warmed up as soon as possible."

"Kyle," Jen asked. "Can you sit up?"

"I think so. Help me."

With considerable pain, Kyle made it to the sitting position. I told him that we were about a half mile from the cabin and that I would have to carry him there. He knew that was the only way. Jen got behind Kyle as I got on all fours and crawled up close to his chest and put my head under one arm. Jen pushed his back toward me as I lifted to stand straight up on two legs. Kyle screamed in pain during this process, but we did not stop. Once I was standing with Kyle draped over my shoulder he became quiet.

"He passed out," Jen said. "I will run back to the cabin and stoke the fire. The cabin should be toasty warm by the time you get there."

"Sounds good," I said. "Grab my rifle, okay? I will come back for the saw and the axe after everything settles down."

A second later, with the rifle in hand, Jen was off and running toward the river. I took one quick look around and then followed the trail Jen had taken. The path to the river did not cause any problems for me, but negotiating my way down the steep bank of the river created some balance issues. Because the bank was collapsing from all the rain, it was also very mucky and slippery. I almost tripped after one of my boots got stuck. That fall would have greatly decreased Kyle's chances for survival because he would have been tossed to the rocks on the river's edge. Luck was on my side, and Kyle's side. At the last fraction of a second, I freed my muddy boot from the quagmire and slammed it in front of me preventing the fall. I stopped for a moment to catch my breath and then ran down the riverside as fast as I could with one hundred and fifty pounds or so on my back.

Jen was waiting for me and swung the door open as I closed the distance between myself and the cabin.

"The bunk is by the stove. I dragged it back over there," she said, as I rushed past her as she was headed toward the stairs. "I have a fire going."

"Excellent!" was all I could get out of my oxygen depleted lungs as I gently laid Kyle on the bunk. He was still out cold, so while Jen was upstairs, I stripped Kyle down naked and then rolled a sheet around him that would serve as pajamas. Jen came downstairs with an extra quilt we had in storage and a couple of pillows. I checked to see if Kyle was breathing, he was. I sat down in a chair next to the stove and started to remove my wet clothes.

"You were amazing out there, Jen!"

"Thanks, I guess that CNA license I earned in high school came in handy."

"You never told me about that."

"I realize that now," she said. "I guess it never came up, and I never needed to use it until now."

"Well, I for one am glad you were with me."

"Thanks. I think he may be hurt worse than we think so I need to check his legs and the rest of his body for more damage. I will need your help."

"Okay, what do you want me to do?"

"Well," Jen said. "We need to roll him to one side so I can see the full length of his backside."

"Should I turn his shoulders while you control his legs?" I asked, cringing a bit at the thought of what we might find.

"Yes, that will work."

Gently, we turned Kyle onto his right shoulder and side. Jen released her grip on his legs after I propped them in place with the extra blanket and a pillow. She then checked him over thoroughly and found no further signs of external injury. We rolled him on his back and covered him up with the blanket. Jen placed her hands on his left leg like a person would who was trying to reach around a tree trunk with her hands. She worked slowly down to his ankle on the first leg. When she was done she said, "Nothing broken in this leg, but I expect that the muscles are torn is several places."

"That is a good thing, considering what could have been wrong," I said.

Jen did not respond. Her focus was on the right leg. I could tell by her demeanor that the injuries to it were much worse. About halfway down the thigh Jen found a break. She worked her hands down the rest of his leg. With her hands gently on his ankle, she announced, "The ankle is shattered."

I knew by of the tone of her voice that it was much worse than either of us had expected. Jen seemed reluctant to remove her hands, as if it would fall to pieces if she did.

"What are we going to do?" I asked.

"Well, to start with, I can set the thigh bone. It felt like a clean break. As for the ankle, there is nothing I can do. He needs surgery, and soon."

"Oh boy, this is bad. I hope that they realize there is a missing plane and send out a search party."

I went to the window and saw that the rain had all but subsided although it was still rather windy. I returned to the bunk where Jen was adjusting Kyle's leg.

After a few minutes of work, Jen looked up. "There," she said. "As long as we do not move him, his thigh bone will be okay."

"Do you need splints?"

"Yes, I need several pieces of your leftover one-inch thick lumber that are at least twelve inches long."

"I have some right outside. I will go get it."

"Good, thanks. While you are doing that I will rip up an old shirt and use it to tie the splints in place. That will have to do until help arrives."

Just as we were finishing the splint, Kyle showed signs of regaining his consciousness. After he opened his eyes, it took him awhile to remember us and even longer to remember what had happened to him. Once we had all of that explained, Kyle started to ask questions about the rest of the crew. We told him what we had seen at the crash site. He fell silent for a long time, so we let him be with his thoughts.

"Kyle, are you in any pain?" Jen asked.

"Yes, some. But it is mainly a dull throbbing in my ankle."

His words reminded me of the bear attack a year ago. After a while the pain was gone but there remained that dull, annoying throbbing that was just on the cusp of being painful.

"Is help on the way?" He finally asked.

"No," I said. "Not that we know of anyway. We have no way to contact the outside world."

"Well, we should have landed in Fairbanks at nine-thirty this morning," Kyle said. "What time is it now?"

"Four in the afternoon," I replied.

A tear rolled down his cheek, as he mumbled something about his wife and baby.

I said to Jen, "They have to be out looking for the plane by now. Too much time has passed for them not to miss a plane."

"Let's hope so. For his sake, they have to get here soon."

Just then we heard a helicopter nearing the cabin. By the time I got outside it was past us and almost over the crash site. I yelled to Jen that I was going to run up there and inform the crew that we have a survivor. I thought about cutting cross country but realized faster time would be made if I followed the path to the river like we had always done. The rain had completely stopped and that made getting to the crash site much easier and faster.

By the time I reached the site, the crew members were scattered about searching the area. The chopper pilot saw me bounding through the grass and alders and raced toward me thinking I was a survivor of the crash. Breathlessly, I introduced myself, telling him that there were two dead people in the cockpit and one survivor who we had carried to the cabin.

"Okay," the pilot said to a crew of men who had gathered behind him. "Check the plane for the two deceased. Be careful. There will be hot spots and jagged metal." When he was done giving instructions, I said,

"Kyle, the guy at our cabin, said there were only three onboard. Do you know if that is correct?"

"Yes," he said very matter of fact tone. "Three total crew members."

"Good, I was worried we might have missed someone during our search."

"What kind of shape is the survivor in?" the crew leader asked.

"As far as we can tell he has a broken leg and a shattered ankle."

"How do you know that?" he questioned.

"Well, sir, my wife is a CNA. We have a cabin downstream about a half mile."

"I know, we flew over it." He said this as he turned and searched for his crew members who had resumed their work around the wreckage.

After a short search he called two men by name and ordered them to get a transport board and any other material they needed to carry the injured man back to the chopper. They responded quickly, and when they had everything they followed me back to the cabin. Kyle was awake. Jen was speaking softly to him as he seemed to be very upset. The two paramedics made a quick assessment of Kyle's condition and then asked Jen a few questions. In quick time they had Kyle's leg in an inflatable splint that went from his crotch down to completely cover his foot. Our makeshift splint and wrapping lay on the floor beside the stove. They rolled him onto the transport board and strapped him snuggly in place. Each man grabbed an end of the board and as I held open the door they headed out toward the chopper.

The helicopter was sitting in the only spot that offered solid, level ground to land on so they had to carry Kyle from the cabin. When we got there the pilot fired up the engines. After Kyle was loaded and secured the pilot took off leaving the others behind to do the cleanup chores. They were well on their way to extracting the two bodies from the wrecked plane. Still, I offered our help, but the commander said they had it covered. That was okay with us. We went back to the cabin to take a well-deserved break from these totally unexpected happenings of the day.

It was seven thirty when we heard the chopper return. It landed in the same spot as it had earlier in the day. We did not go up there. At this point we figured if they wanted any information from us, they knew where to find us. That they did. About an hour later the crew chief knocked on the cabin door. Jen answered the door and invited him in. He came in and asked us what we saw. Together, we told the story as it had played out from the very beginning. He said that the people responsible for investigating accidents like this would be around in the next couple of days and may want to ask us more questions. We told him that we were fine with that.

After he left the cabin, and the chopper took off, it was back to the peace and quiet that we loved. Jen and I were shaken by the day's events. What had happened was so out of character for this place. Of all the places a plane could crash, it crashed in our backyard. I know it was an accident, but it felt like an invasion. This occurrence helped us realize that we were a private family, and that we really treasured that part of our lives.

"I wonder what the next few days will bring our direction." I asked Jen in a tired voice.

"Just like he said, more people."

"Well, beyond all else," I said. "I hope Kyle is okay. He was banged up pretty bad, and was frightened for the well-being of his family."

"Me too. While you were outside he told me about his wife and baby. They live in Fairbanks."

"I bet they were worried. Hopefully his family knows that he is okay now."

"He is one lucky guy," Jen went on to say. "I find it unbelievable that he did not die. He did not tell me how he made it through but am interested in that story when he comes back to visit."

"Did he say he was going to come back?" I asked.

"Yes," Jen said. "After he heals he said that he and his family will come out and thank us properly."

"That will be nice."

"Well, Honey, it is ten o'clock. I am ready for bed."

"Me too," Jen answered tiredly.

I took Jen's hand in mine and we climbed the stairs in silence. It was still daylight out so no lamp was needed. I remember nothing beyond my head hitting the pillow. Lights out!

## Chapter 3
## July Is a Great Month

The first week of July passed just as we figured it would. There were all kinds of official looking people up and down the beach. A couple of crews came by boat. The last person to leave stopped by the cabin and told us that if the contents of the plane were still there in ninety days, we were free to take and use what we wanted. That sounded like a great deal to us. With that he left. Once again, peace and quiet descended on our cabin home.

The next morning, I glanced at the calendar and realized that Aunt Alice was due to visit in a week. This gave us plenty of time to work on a list of chores that needed doing. First on the list was fire wood. Jen and I concentrated on that task as much as possible. We cut everything close to the cabin and carried it back in the largest chunks we could handle. This was exhausting work, but would save valuable time in the winter. We also took a couple day-long excursions along our trap line trails to cut and stack eight-foot sections that I could throw in the sled during the winter months and haul back to the cabin. In a week's time we had enough wood cut to last us three quarters of the way through the winter.

Finally, the day arrived for Aunt Alice's visit. We were very excited to see her and to welcome her to our new home. Just like clockwork we heard the buzz of an outboard motor from down river. Alice said she would be here early in the morning, and she kept that promise.

Jen took off at a full run to the river, waving her arms the entire way. Aunt Alice was in the boat with her nephews, John and Andy. Even though she knew the river as well as anyone, they did not want her to travel the river by herself.

"Hello," Alice yelled from the boat. "How are you two doing?"

"Great!" We chimed in unison.

"Hi Andy, Hello John, did you guys have a good trip?"

"Yes," answered Andy. "It was smooth sailing the entire way."

"Excellent."

After they beached the boat Alice slowly made her way to the front of the craft where Jen and I each took a hand and helped her to the ground.

"Thank you," she said, as we both received a bear hug at the same time.

"It is so good to see you, Auntie. How have you been?" asked Jen.

"I am doing okay. I miss your uncle."

"I do too, Auntie. I think of him every day."

John and Andy had arm loads of supplies. They jumped to the ground and set down the bundles to meet my extended hand with theirs. We shook hands and stood there talking for a few minutes. Jen and Alice headed to the cabin so I grabbed everything that I could carry and followed after them. As we topped the hill above the river, John and Andy saw the cabin.

"Wow, you did some major building this summer," said Andy.

John then asked, "Did you two do all the work?"

"Yes, Jen and I did every last bit of the work. We put in long hours. There is still a lot to do, but most of it can wait until winter."

"Nice!"

"Thanks guys. Come on in and I will show you around."

Inside the cabin we wandered around and talked for about an hour. It was so nice for Jen and me to show off all that we had accomplished. Presenting our home to our loved ones made it feel special. It was our goal from the very beginning of our relationship to make a house into a home.

Having friends and family share our space added to that concept. Everyone loved the upstairs bedroom and all the windows. Finally, it seemed that we had shown everything to show. I headed back to the boat to grab some of the remaining items that needed to be in the cabin. John and Andy accompanied me.

"This is a great looking boat. I always wanted to talk to Alvin about it. I need a boat."

"There are boats for sale all the time in Fairbanks," John responded. "I can get you a good deal from the place where I work."

"On a new boat and motor?" I asked.

"Yes, new or used."

"I wonder if Jen would be up for a trip into town. I remember she has mentioned several times how nice it would be to have a boat."

"We were hoping you guys wanted to come back for a week or so because the Sockeye salmon are running strong in the Copper River. It would also be a great time to check out boats."

"Dang, yes. I heard about the salmon from that river."

Andy jumped in the conversation and explained how they set up camp to smoke and can salmon on the spot.

"By the time we leave there, all of our salmon will be processed to our liking; that is, except for the ones we save for the grill or the oven."

"I am in. I bet Jen will be too. Let's go back to the cabin and see what she thinks."

My excitement was piqued. When we arrived at the cabin, Jen and Aunt Alice were frying bacon and eggs. Buttered toast already graced the table. I grabbed a slice and gave Jen a peck on the cheek.

"Want to go on a fishing trip?" I asked.

"Yes. We can leave tomorrow."

"So, you and Alice talked about it already?"

"Yes, we did. It sounds like an excellent idea. You know I have been there before, right?"

"Yes, I assumed that since everyone but me is familiar with the place."

We talked about the details over breakfast. John and Andy had several nets for this type of fishing, and Alice had several more that Alvin had used over many years of fishing salmon. We would have to buy some camping equipment if the trip was to be comfortable for everyone. We reasoned that any cost incurred this year would eventually be spread out over many years of fishing on the Copper. Aunt Alice had several canners, so we would leave ours at the cabin. Still, we would need canning supplies like salt, pepper, sugar, and jars. A lot of jars, I hoped.

The plans were made. The rest of the day Jen spent packing clothes and other items we would need for the trip. Andy and John helped me with some building work that needed to be completed.

After that, we walked up to the crash site and checked it out. The scene was a bit bizarre. I felt a little strange rummaging through the cargo that was stacked in the tail section. We did not stay long, but did see some things we wanted if they were not claimed. Overall, it was a great day. That night Alice had her comfortable bed under the stairs, while John and Andy had planned ahead and brought their air mattresses which were laid out on the floor of our addition. We were all home.

Upstairs Jen and I discussed the upcoming events and what needed to be bought in Fairbanks to bring back out here. We decided it would be best to get most of our winter shopping done on this trip in case we could not get in later in the summer. Living this far from civilization had already taught us that we always needed to plan ahead. As a final thought,

I said, "We need to get you a snow machine and a sled, and we have to get my machine out here.

"Do you think they will both fit in your new boat?" Jen asked with her beautiful, teasing smile.

"Yes," I replied. "I think they will."

"Good night, Jen."

"Good night, Codi."

# Chapter 4
## Salmon Galore

Early the next morning we were well on our way to Fairbanks. The whole crew was excited because the salmon were running heavily this year and the quotas for individual catches were higher than usual. Once we reached the boat launch area in Fairbanks we made quick work of putting the boat on the trailer. We went straight back to Alice's house and loaded up all the equipment needed for the trip. I could tell that they were sure that we would join them because everything was all figured out. After that we stopped at a huge outdoor store where I bought camping gear and cots. The last stop was the grocery store where we loaded up on food, water, and canning supplies, mainly jars.

Soon we were cruising down the highway toward Copper Center. It would take us at least seven hours to get to the fishing spot. Once we reached Chitina, we would be within a couple miles of the camping area. There was one spot at the site that Andy and John kept talking about. They hoped no one was there. As they explained it to me, there was a clump of trees in the middle of an open area very close to the river. It would offer us shade if the temperatures got too warm and was out of the way of most of the bear traffic which focused around the fish cleaning station, which sat about one hundred yards away.

The road from Chitina to the campground was interesting to say the least. It was narrow and high above the fast-moving, brown water river. At some points it looked like the road would crumble under the weight of the truck and we would go over the edge. To save my sanity I had a tight grip on the door handle while focusing my eyes on the bank on the other side of the road. That was not the worst part, however. Right before the campground there is a steep decline that leads to the parking lot. Going down we did not need four-wheel drive, but I knew for sure that we would need it going back up. There were a great many loose rocks on the road, some the size of baseballs. I had a momentary vision of us rolling backwards and crashing at the bottom of the harrowingly steep incline.

The camping spot we wanted was open. I knew this by Andy's whooping call of excitement.

"Yeeha!" Andy's yell scared the you know what out of me.

"Yeah Buddy, we have the prime set up," said John.

Andy pulled the truck up close to the trees so that the truck was between us and the rest of the campers. We had the entire mountain range view and river view from the tent site.

"This is excellent," I said. "Everything is just as we planned."

"Yes," said Alice, "we have spent a lot of time here and have caught thousands of salmon over the years."

"This is a tradition I could get used to," I told her in a thankful tone.

"Well, Codi, from this point forward you are part of our family so it is your tradition, too."

"Thanks, Alice. That means a great deal to me, especially since my family never did anything like this."

We finished our conversation, and after a short walk around that helped to familiarize me with the area, we started to set up camp. It was late in the afternoon and as we worked we would periodically see fishermen coming out of the woods that lead downstream, most of them carrying a tub of fish between them. Some of them had 4-wheelers with trailers. That, I thought, was the best set up. After we had the majority of the camp completed, I wandered over to the fish cleaning station where a teenage boy was struggling to clean his fish.

"Hello," I said as I admiringly stared at his fish. "It looks like the fishing was good."

"Yes, it was," he replied, "but cleaning these fish is a chore."

"May I help you?" I asked.

"Sure."

"I am not the best, but have become quite handy at cleaning all kinds of fish."

He looked at me with a friendly smile, and then handed me his knife. I gave the knife a once over with my eyes and could see it was terribly dull. I set it down and trotted back to our camp to get my sharpening steel. I returned to the cleaning station and gave the knife a dozen strokes or so on each side of the blade. Now it was sharp and we could get some work done.

"Do you want these filleted?" I asked.

"Yes, please."

"I do not want to make you feel bad, but you caught a lot of fish yet you don't seem to know how to clean them. Why is that?"

"I know," he replied. "I used to come here with my grandpa, but he died when I was ten. I used to watch him, but really never learned how to clean fish on my own."

"Okay, today I will teach you and then you will know how to clean fish for the rest of your life. I will start cleaning them while you go over and ask that nice lady in the blue jacket for another fillet knife."

"Okay, I will be right back."

When he got back with the knife I had three fish cleaned, the fillets resting in cold water.

"That knife is sharp" I said. "Be careful. Come stand next to me and do as I do."

He sauntered over and said, "Okay, I am ready."

He was a quick learner. He followed my lead on the first fish, and on the second one, the knowledge he gained from watching his grandfather must have kicked in because he went on his own pace after that. After a few small nicks from the knife blades, two for him and one for me, we had the fish ready to be bagged.

"What is your name?" I asked.

"Colt."

"Nice to meet you, Colt. I am Codi. How old are you?"

"I am seventeen."

Are you here by yourself?"

"Yes."

"Are you camping?"

"Yes."

"Would you like to join us for supper?"

"I would like that a lot. We can have fresh Sockeye, my treat." He said with a smile on his face.

"Well then, let's head back to my camp."

We grabbed all of our belongings and carried them across the lot and into the trees by the truck.

"Hey everyone, this is Colt."

"Hello Colt," The whole group said at once.

"Colt is going to join us for supper and he is supplying the fish, fresh fish."

"Oh darn," Jen said. "I wanted a Spam sandwich." To which everyone responded with hearty laughter.

"Ha-ha," I replied. "I do not believe that for a second."

"You are so right. I thought we would have to wait until tomorrow night for a fish supper."

Colt dug five big fillets out of his cooler. Aunt Alice graciously took them and laid them on her waiting cookie sheets. The fire was built and the grate to hold the pans was in place. They were sizzling only minutes after the flames began licking the bottom of the pans. The smell was incredible. In a pot next to the fish, Alice and Jen had prepared a seasoned wild rice mix, and next to that a huge pot of canned corn was beginning to bubble. Supper looked good.

We sat down to eat just as the sun went behind the mountains. There was a lot of daylight left but the sun would be gone from our view until the next morning. The temperature dropped and I could see that Alice was cold. A couple of blankets from one of the tents draped over her legs and around her shoulders cured that. Soon after supper was over, Colt grabbed his cooler and walked the thirty yards to his truck. He had a topper on it and spent his nights sleeping there. It made a great tent.

We sat around the fire for a couple more hours talking about tomorrow's activities. If the fish were running strong, there would be plenty of work and fun for everyone. We were all excited for the morning. I kissed Jen goodnight and then retired to the tent I shared with John and Andy. We all slept well.

I woke up to Andy snoring. It was light out and a quick check of my watch told me it was four-thirty. There was some rumbling outside by the fire pit. I hoped it was not a bear. My worries were squelched when I heard Jen say to Alice that she was ready to make toast, and that we better roust the guys from their sleep.

"I am awake, I said, trying to make it sound like I was up and moving.

"Well, then come on out, breakfast is ready."

I hadn't fooled Jen. She knew I was still in my sleeping bag. Even though I was warm and comfortable, the thought of hot coffee, a warm breakfast, and tubs full of salmon made it impossible for me to stay put. In a matter of minutes, I was outside sipping that coffee. John and Andy were close behind me. After breakfast we did a quick clean up and then gathered all of our equipment. The sun was peeking over the mountains as we entered the woods following the trail to our fishing spot.

It was a short walk, no more than a quarter mile. The easy part of the walk was over. We stood overlooking the river from a grassy spot about three hundred feet above river level. In front of us was what John and Andy called the goat trail. It was a winding path that went back and forth on its way down the hillside. It looked treacherous, and probably was if a person did not pay attention to the task at hand.

"Keep one hand on the bank for balance," John instructed, "and don't look down," he then said with short, nervous laugh.

"Okay," I said, as I looked around.

Everyone seemed to be enjoying my anxious state of mind. The four of them broke out in laughter and the joke was over.

"It is quite easy." John told me, "Just make sure of where your feet are at and you will be fine. The hardest part is coming up with fifteen eight to ten-pound red salmon in your tub."

"Okay," I said, "let's get going."

John led the way and I followed him. We made it down in no time at all. It was an easy walk, not worth any of the fear I had at first let take over my mind. At the bottom along the river there were many big boulders that we would rest against as we held our dip nets in the eddy. An eddy is a spot in the current where the water changes direction and flows upstream for a short way. The salmon like this because it makes their journey upstream less strenuous. It also creates the perfect spot to put in a dip net to catch these beautiful fish. There were no other people on this part of the river so we spread out and claimed our spots. Jen and I found an eddy about fifty yards upstream from the others, a place where we could sit side by side and still control the long handles of the nets as they rested in the stream. We got situated and placed our nets in the spot we thought would hold the most fish. It was slow, not what we had expected. We looked downstream every once in a while, but saw that no one else was enjoying action either.

"Do we have coffee?" I asked Jen.

"Yes, two Thermoses full. Would you like some?"

"I would."

"Okay, be right back."

In a few minutes, Jen was back with coffee for two.

"Here you go."

"Thanks."

I put the cup to my lips and at the same time felt a thump in my net. I found a spot and quickly set down my coffee. With a great effort and a couple grunts, I pulled the net in. Nothing.

"Too slow." Jen laughed.

She jumped up. I could tell she felt a thump in her net. Like an old professional, Jen pulled the net handle in until she had the hoop part of the net in her hands and expertly hoisted three large Sockeye to the sand between the rocks.

"That's how you do it."

"Dang, was all I could say. Then, "I definitely picked the right girl to be my wife."

"Wrong, I picked you and worked my charms."

"Oh, is that how it went?"

"Yup, and now look where you are."

"I like it," I said as I bent down to subdue the flopping salmon and get them on the stringer and back in the water to keep them alive as long as possible.

"They are huge," Jen said.

"What do you think, about ten pounds each?"

"Close to that," Jen replied.

The commotion caught the attention of Alice and her nephews. They were watching us when both John and Andy turned toward the water to work some fish that had just hit their nets.

"Looks like the run is on," said Aunt Alice from her perch on a low setting rock.

From that point on, the fishing was fast and furious. Because of the high numbers of fish running this year the limit was adjusted from fifteen fish to a total of twenty-five fish per person. When we decided to call it quits for the day, it was close to noon and we had somewhere around one hundred fish. We ate a quick lunch of sandwiches and chips that Jen and Alice had packed. After that we placed some fish in plastic bags and then put the bags in old camping backpacks. Andy, John, and I each carried a pack full of fish on our back. Jen and Alice carried the nets while John and I did double duty and shared a tub full of fish between us. It was a hard climb to the top. When we got there, we took a well-deserved rest.

After ten or fifteen minutes of sitting on the green grass and in the warm sunshine everyone had caught their breath and was ready to make the final walk to camp. Back at camp we all jumped in and started to clean fish with the exception of Alice. She wanted to get the canners ready so we could run a couple batches yet today. I was impressed with the fish cleaning skills of my wife and her cousins. Even though I was quite good by this time, they took the meat off of a fish at least twice as fast as I did.

Our catch for the day was an impressive ninety-one fish. We cut all of these into canning sized chunks, most of them with the skin on. Jen reminded me that the skin on the Sockeye salmon is thin and tasty. We took the tub of cleaned fish over to Alice and she immediately began packing pint jars. Along with the fish she added salt, pepper, and to some of the jars, she added a healthy squirt of catsup. She caught me watching her as she was adding this last ingredient.

"You will love it," she said. "It was Alvin's favorite."

"Oh, I know I will like it. The pairing seems to fit well, fish and catsup, especially after it is cooked."

We were silent for a bit. Alice was engaged in her work and I stood there taking it all in. In a way I wished I had the opportunities to do things like this when I was a kid. But, then again, I thought, maybe it would not be as special as it is now.

Alice broke the silence and my trance when she asked me to get the fish bellies from the cleaning station.

"Okay," I said. "What do you want me to do with them?"

"Well, when you get them over here, I am going to add this brown sugar and salt. In the morning we are going to smoke them."

I was off like a streak of lightning. Learning how to smoke fish was high on my priority list. As I was carrying the fish across the parking lot, I realized we did not have a smokehouse with us.

"Where is the smokehouse, Alice?"

"Right there," she said, "laying at your feet."

I looked down at four 4x4 sheets of plywood that had a definite layer of smoke on them. Next to the wood was a pile of old oven racks and a bundle of rebar.

"I get it, this is our smokehouse. Assembly required?" I asked.

"Yes," Alice answered. "Are you volunteering?"

"Yes I am."

About twenty feet from the tents and the truck, I set up the smokehouse. It was a simple, yet, I could see, a very effective little structure. Once I had the walls in place I put the rebar through the pre-drilled holes. The rebar served as supports to lay the oven racks on top of. The top of the smokehouse was a piece of plywood that was about 5x5 feet and had a hole for a smokestack to go in. On the opposite side from the smoke stack hole, there was another hole that looked like another piece of stove pipe would fit in to.

"Why is this hole here, Alice?"

"To connect the stove where the smoke will come from."

"Oh, okay. Where is that at?"

"Sitting on the tailgate. The two sections of stove pipe are there too."

"Okay, thanks."

With a few more minutes of work, I had the smokehouse figured out and put together. In the meantime, Alice and Jen salted and sugared the fish bellies and put them in a cooler that had been filled with ice that we bought at a gas station on the trip down. Everyone was busy doing jobs that needed to be done in fish camp. By the time the first two batches were building pressure in the pressure canners, it was seven in the evening. The day had flown by. Alice used the same type of propane burners that I had at our cabin. They worked great and were easy to control the heat in order to keep the proper pressure in the canners. Alice figured we could get two batches done before we retired for the day.

No one was too keen on cooking supper so we had Spam sandwiches and chips, the same food as we had for lunch. It was a great way to end the day. The air was cool and the fire was warm. My eyes were heavy from the day of work. I dozed off in my camp chair and dreamed of Pretty Girl. After what seemed to be only seconds of sleep, Jen woke me up and we all turned in for the night. I hoped my little bear was okay.

## Chapter 5
## More Fish

The next morning, we were all up early, and everyone seemed well-rested. The plan was that I, along with John and Andy, would go back and catch thirty-four more fish. That would give us enough for everyone to have what they needed for the year. Alice and Jen would stay back and finish the canning and get the fish bellies in the smoke house. The extended plan was to leave the following morning and finish any leftover chores in Fairbanks. During our time in the city, Jen and I would purchase a boat and motor, a snow machine, and do our winter shopping.

On the way to our fishing spot we met up with Colt. He was by the fish cleaning station doing some final cleanup work before heading home. We chatted for a while and hoped that we would meet up here next year. After our goodbyes were said we hiked the trail to our favorite spot. Each of us had our own net and a backpack. If we caught fish it would be a much easier day than the day before.

At the bottom of the goat trail we encountered an old man who had been there all night. He had a small campfire burning, and a stringer of twelve or fifteen fish. He told us he hoped for a few more. We scattered out down the riverside and put our nets in the water. There was a continuous eddy that ran about one hundred feet along the bank. It seemed the perfect spot. It was. As soon as our nets found their spots in the stream the fish slammed them. In one hour, we had our fish and we were hiking up the trail. The old man did well, also, so we helped him out by carrying some of his fish back to camp.

Alice and Jen were surprised to see us so soon. They could tell by our heavily laden packs that the fishing was good. We cleaned the fish and put them on ice. The fish bellies that were being smoked smelled delicious. I asked Alice if they were ready to sample.

"Well, she said, "They are not done, but if you will open the lid and grab five or six pieces, I will make them ready to sample."

"Sounds like a plan," I said.

I did as she instructed, and when I returned to the fire pit area where everyone was gathered and enjoying the warm fire, Alice had a cast iron pan heating over the open flames. I handed her the partially smoked bellies and she plopped them in the hot pan. The sizzle was immediate. Alice let them cook for about one minute and then flipped them over. She placed a cover on the pan and removed it from the fire.

"There," she said, "the samples will be ready in ten minutes."

"They smell absolutely delicious," I said.

It was a great day to sit around the fire and drink coffee and discuss our adventure. We would enjoy one more night at the camp site and then head home. I got up after a bit and removed the lid from the pan. Steam came out when I did this so I knew they were too hot to eat but after a couple of minutes they cooled enough to give them a try.

"These are wonderful, Alice. I love the sweet, salty taste with the smoke flavor mixed in."

Everyone got up and sampled the fish. Judging by the silence that overtook the group, the bellies were a success.

"We will can some of these when we get to my place," Alice said. "That way you and Jen can take a dozen jars home with you to enjoy throughout the winter."

"Sweet, thank you!"

The day ended as it had begun, fun and relaxing. We packed up everything we could before going to bed so that the next morning would be spent taking care of the tents and other small packing jobs that would need doing.

## Chapter 6
## So Many Boats

My interests shifted from fish to boats. The day after we returned to Fairbanks, I went along with John to his workplace to check out the boat selection. Jen and Alice went to the bank where Jen withdrew enough money to buy all that we needed for winter supplies.

At the boat dealership, I was immediately attracted to an eighteen-foot Hewes Craft boat with a one hundred fifty horse outboard motor on it. The boat and motor were used, and the salesperson informed me that the motor was blown and that the owner decided to sell the boat rather than have it fixed. The boat itself was in like new condition. The motor had suffered costly, yet repairable damage after the owner did some work on it and did not put it together correctly, which had deprived the engine of oil. The salesman said it would be best to purchase a new motor. The boat itself would be a steal because its owner was fed up with his losses and wanted the boat sold as soon as possible.

There were several motors that would be a good fit for this boat. We talked about the shallow water in the river and what the best way was to get around that. The salesperson said he would go with a one hundred and fifty horse Mercury motor that would come with the standard prop and also with a Jet Stream set up for extremely shallow water. John and I talked it over and concluded that it was an awesome deal. With the new motor and the great condition that the boat was in, we would have a solid rig for many years to come. That was good enough for me. I got everything settled financially. The salesman said my boat would be ready in two days. At that time, we would go for a test run on the river where I would learn all I needed to know about operating a boat of this size.

As we were going through the purchase process, I realized that the boat was not big enough to carry our snow machines, but it would do well for everything else. I would have to hire the same boat operator who delivered my lumber to do the same for the snow machines. After leaving the dealership I began to wonder about freeze up and what I would do with the boat. It staying in the river during the winter months was not an option. I would not have a boat after ice out. John suggested that I buy a dock system that would allow me to lift the boat out of the water and pull it up the bank. Lifting it out of the water was the easy part, but that would not be enough. I would have to get it above the floodplain so the whole rig did not get swept downstream. The rig he had in mind would cover all my needs, but pulling it up the bank was another issue.

The best option was for me to buy a generator and an electric winch which we would mount on a ten inch by ten inches by ten-foot green treated timber. We would bury the pole as deep as possible in the ground and then securely mount the winch to the front of the pole. As long as I had enough cable, we figured this would work perfectly. John got all of this stuff lined up through his work. The owner gave me a nice deal on everything because of the amount of money we spent at his shop. I finished my day by securing the boat and the driver who would deliver my load to our cabin.

Jen and Alice were at home. They wanted to go out to eat. Alice said it was her treat.

"Where do you all want to eat," asked Alice.

"It makes no difference to me," I said.

Everyone else was open to just about anything. We decided to go north of town to a little brewery that served a good burger and fries. While we ate we discussed our fishing trip and how many pints of fish we canned.

"Three hundred and four pints," Alice proudly announced. "Plus, we have all of the fish bellies smoked and canned, and we have all the fish you guys caught on the last day put in the freezer."

"Wow, what a fishing trip. We will have all the salmon we need for a year or more." I said.

"Jen joined the conversation, saying, "If the fishing is bad next year we will have some to get us through."

John agreed, "I don't think we will need near as many next year because of the catch this year."

After supper we went back to Alice's house. Jen and I began packing up our share of the fish and put them in the garage along with the supplies she had bought earlier in the day. We had quite the stockpile of dried and canned food. We bought very little canned meat because we now had so much fish, and we still had canned moose meat from last year. We did buy some canned fruit, but would rely more on blueberries this year. Their abundance was endless. The bulk of our food was canned vegetables. Someday, we hoped to have a garden that would allow us to grow most of our food. Of course, the essentials like coffee, tea, sugar, salt, flour, yeast, and spices would likely always have to be purchased.

The remaining two days in Fairbanks passed slowly, partly because of the anticipation of wanting to drive the new boat. Mostly, however, because I missed our home. Its solitude was amazing, and the contradiction of city life was alarming. There were so many noises that I had grown un-accustomed to hearing. The constant noise of traffic was one thing I did not miss. The other issue I had was that there were people everywhere and they were always on the go. The longer we stayed in town, the more we became like the people we did not want to be.

We loved our time with the family. It was so nice to see that Alice was getting along without Alvin. They had been very close. John and Andy had really stepped up and were there to help her with anything that she needed. On the morning we were to leave, I made the trip to buy a new snow machine for Jen. I also bought two single place trailers and asked if one of the shop men could deliver the trailers to Alice's house. They agreed to do so, and said the trailers would be there before noon. Everything was lined up. John and Andy were at work when we left, so I instructed Alice that one trailer was for John and one was for Andy, and, that each one was to get either Alvin's snow machine or Bill's snow machine. Both were stored in Alice's garage. She was totally taken aback by the gesture, but said the boys would be extremely happy. That was all I needed to hear.

Jen and I both went out with the boat salesman, mostly because Jen was experienced in handling a boat, so she could be a co-teacher for me and get a refresher course for herself. It was a pretty simple process. We finished up in about an hour, and that included a nice run up the river at full speed. The boat was impressive and would serve us well for hunting and general transportation. Alice was waiting for us at the landing. We had packed everything in John's truck, and now packed all of our goods into the new boat. It was getting late, so we said a tearful goodbye to Alice and headed out to our cabin home.

Chapter Seven
Home for the Winter

It was a fun trip out. We took turns driving the boat, and were very pleased with our purchase. Within a week we would have the snow machines, generator, and the dock system delivered. Plus, there were a few more things that I bought that were special for my wife. On the boat with the rest of our supplies would be a second stove to go in the addition, and everything I needed to build an indoor shower. Jen would be pleased. Buying the boat and other essentials created a great deal more work for me, so before the delivery arrived there was a lot of prep work that needed to be completed.

Just as I finished my thinking about all the work that needed doing, we rounded the last bend in the river before our cabin, and there on the beach stood a grizzly. Even though my heart began pounding at the sight, I recognized her within a second or two. It was Pretty Girl. I wondered if she heard us coming and came down to meet us, or had this been a simple coincidence. She had gained weight and looked good. We pulled up right where she was waiting. She made me laugh right away by displaying her toughness with those little huffs and snorts that she had done since the first day we were together. She seemed to miss us. I playfully patted her behind after I jumped out of the boat.

"You are a tough one, aren't you," I said to her.

She turned to look at the boat when Jen greeted her.

"Hey Pretty Girl. How have you been? We have treats for you."

"Oh, yes, I saved you some salmon heads and some livers and skin."

We had her goodies packed on ice and it was likely that they would still be frozen because they spent a few days in Alice's freezer. Pretty Girl did not seem to be overly impressed with our emptying out the boat, but she was in the way.

"Hey, Jen," I said. "Which cooler are the fish heads in?"

"The blue one she is sniffing at and trying to pry open."

"Okay, thanks. I am going to give her the treats. That should keep her occupied and out of the way for a while."

I opened the cooler and pulled out a bag that had about ten pounds of prime fish remains in it. They were partially thawed so I carried the bag to the side and about twenty feet from the boat and dumped them on the rocks. Pretty Girl began eating instantly and, as expected, remained out of our way until the work was done. We had enough time to carry everything up to the cabin because even canned food was not safe from a hungry bear.

It was great to be home. We left the cabin door open while we put things away. After a few minutes, Pretty Girl joined us. She lay contentedly in the doorway with only her head in the cabin. I sat and watched her for a while. Her facial expressions were comical. Her eyes followed Jen as she went back and forth across the cabin floor. She seemed to be genuinely interested in what was going on around her. Eventually, my joy of watching her turned to concern. I hoped she was not being hassled by any male bears. It was breeding season, but she was too young to be bred. The next summer would be the safest time for her to encounter the big, rough male bears. For now, I hoped she was safe. By the time we got everything situated for the night it was ten o'clock. Light was fading fast. We noticed how quickly the days were getting shorter. This was the reminder that we needed to let us know winter was on its way.

My excitement was too much for me to hold my secret. As Jen and I lay in bed enjoying the moonlight softly lighting our room, I told her about the shower and the new stove. She was overjoyed, but then questioned me, thinking I might be pulling her leg.

"Are you teasing me?" she asked.

"No, I knew you wanted a shower, and with the materials I bought I can build one for you."

"You are so sweet. Thank you. What a wonderful thing for you to do."

"Only the best for my wife."

"I love you."

"I love you, too."

"Good night."

"Good night."

Chapter 8
The Work Begins

Early the next morning I was up and drinking coffee and making a list of everything that needed doing. I prioritized so that the inside work could be done over the winter in case we ran out of time before snow blanketed the ground and the frigid temperatures set in. The outside work took priority. I could not do much with the boat and dock situation except to level the bank so that it was a gradual decline rather than how it was now, which was more like a dirt bank that we had pounded footsteps into. I grabbed a shovel and walked to the river edge. After checking out the boat to make sure it was tied up solidly, I began digging out the bank. After I was finished I stood back and examined my work. It looked pretty good, kind of like an unpaved boat ramp. Stacked alongside the cabin, I had a significant pile of leftover lumber, and there were some dried, branchless trees laying on the beach that were deposited there as the water retreated this past spring. I stepped off the distance that I figured the length of the logs needed to be, and then ran back to the cabin to get the chainsaw and a couple eight foot two by fours. Back at the beach I cut the logs to length and rolled them over the rocks to get them close to the ramp that I was constructing.

As I struggled to pull them up to the ramp area, Jen appeared and asked if I wanted help.

"Yes, I do. Are you offering?"

"I am."

"Well, see if you can lift that small end. If you can, we will carry it up this incline."

She handled the small end of each log with ease. Jen's help made the entire project so much easier, and it saved a lot of valuable time.

I knew the wheels on the boat lift where eleven feet apart. I measured out eleven feet at each end of the logs and then dug alongside each of the logs so that I had a ditch running the entire length of each one. Then, I rolled each log in the ditch so that it would be level with the ground after they were buried. This was best so that during high water they would be less likely to be carried away in the current. My hope was that this ramp would make it easier on the winch when it pulled the boat and the lift out of the water. I was satisfied for now. This work could be fine-tuned after the lift arrived.

I was so involved in my work that I had completely forgotten about eating breakfast. I knew Jen would have something ready when I got back to the cabin. She did. We had smoked salmon bellies on pilot crackers with a side of baked beans.

"I think I ate too much." I said as I swallowed the last bite of fish.

"Ha-ha," Jen replied. I was wondering where you were putting all that food."

"It was so good and I was very hungry. I think I will go stretch out in the sun by the fire pit."

"Would you like to join me?"

"I think I would," she said with a smile.

We spent a few hours out there in the warm sunshine just talking and laughing and planning.

"Well," I finally said, "I better get back to work."

"What are you going to do now?"

"Start on the woodshed," I said.

"Oh jeez...I forgot all about that."

"Me too," I said with a nervous laugh. "Until just now, it escaped all of my plans, but we really need it to be up before winter. This is the perfect time to get started."

"I will help you."

"Okay, let's get to it."

We gathered up all the tools we would need and walked to the site were the shed would be built.

"The first thing to do is measure out where we want the corner posts to be dug into the ground. It is the same technique we used on the addition."

"Okay," Jen said. "Where do you want the first corner to be?"

"Right where you are standing. That whole area is flat and is close enough to the cabin so we can get wood easily."

It took us about an hour to get everything measured out and then we began digging the holes. We planned that the front of the woodshed would be eight feet high and the back end would be six feet high. The shed plans called for it to be sixteen feet deep and thirty-two feet wide. We had all of the materials delivered with the cabin materials so everything we needed was here. Now, we had to do the actual work. By the end of the day we had all fifteen posts planted in the ground. Because there was still daylight, while Jen went in to make supper, I nailed all the framing boards on that would serve as the outline for the roof. Before I went in for supper, I stood back and admired our work. I found it amazing at how much we could accomplish in one day of hard work.

The next morning, I began working on the shed right away. The first job was to place the two by four cross member pieces in the roof frame we had completed the night before. Once they were done, the frame work would be complete and give added support to the roof. Over that I would nail sheets of tin. This project took me the entire day. The roof was not perfect, but would serve our purpose perfectly. Underneath, there was enough space for a good portion of a winter's supply of wood and space for both snow machines. The entire job took three days. The third day found us stacking our entire wood supply in the shed. Even though all of the wood was under the roof, it would not be enough for winter. Everything else we needed was cut and stacked in the woods and would be gathered after the first snow fell.

We were running short on time as far as July was concerned. The end of the month was near. August would be dedicated to berry picking and brushing trails for the trap lines. If at all possible, I wanted to have the shower built and the wood stove installed by the first week of August. I hoped the delivery of our dock system would be here in the next day or two.

I knew Jen was hard at work. She was in and out of the cabin all day, washing jars and prepping everything we needed for the berries. It was a good day. During supper we talked about Kyle and hoped that everything was going well for him and his family. After that discussion we decided that after breakfast the next day we would walk up to the crash site and rummage through what was still packed in the broken off plane section. We felt better about looking through things now. Right after the crash it seemed strange that we would want anything from such a disaster. But, over a few weeks of talking about the offer that the rescue commander made, it only made sense that we use what we could. Of course, we would not be able to claim anything for a couple months, but that did not mean we couldn't check things out. After all, there was a 4-wheeler sitting up there. It looked pretty beat up after going through the crash, but it would prove useful in many ways if it ran well, or I could fix what needed fixing.

It was raining when we woke up the next morning, so we took it easy in the cabin drinking coffee and eating breakfast. We also did some small inside jobs to include deciding on where the stove and shower would be installed. The plan for the shower was simple. I bought a six-gallon stainless-steel carboy that could be placed on the stove top to heat the shower water. Also included in the setup was a length of steel cable, a couple of medium length logging chains, and a heavy-duty track system that came with a hook, mounted to the bottom of a wheel assembly that ran the length of the track system. I would mount the track on the rafters that spanned the addition and put bolts in the pre-drilled holes on each end to keep it from sailing off either end. The track would begin directly center over the stove and end directly center over the shower stall. The track was eight feet long so we had some options as far as distance between the shower and the stove was concerned. The carboy would be lifted and lowered by a double pulley system that would reduce the muscle power of lifting a full carboy of water by at least half. We would pull the carboy back and forth on the track with a simple length of rope. After we decided the shower stall would stand in the corner of the addition right where it connected to the kitchen area, we knew where the stove had to be. Our plans were made. Now all we needed was the material.

It was still raining lightly after we had finished all the inside chores, but we decided it would be a good time to walk up to the crash site. We donned our raingear and I grabbed the rifle and we were off. We stopped and looked the boat over. Our main concern was water level, and along with that, we worried that critters, to include Pretty Girl and others of her kind, might find it an appealing option for a home and move in. So far, the boat was safe.

For some reason the crashed plane looked like it was there for years. The burn marks were starting to grow new cover. What looked like fireweed plants were growing in the area that had burned. We did not go near the cockpit end of the plane. The sight of the two burned pilots was fresh in our memory and we did not want to re-freshen what we had seen on the crash day. The back end of the airplane is where all the cargo was that had amazingly stayed relatively intact. Still, there were a great deal of damaged items strewn about. Considering the violence of the crash, that was to be expected. After a short inspection from the ground, I stepped up and into the plane and started to move a few of the loose items around to see what was there. Jen did the same thing on the other side. After she removed a couple tie down straps she said,

"Hey, look at this, it is a high chair for infants."

"Oh good, just what we need. I am tired of the kids sitting on the floor at supper time." I smirked.

"Ha-ha," she teased. "You never know. They could be useful in the future."

"I love your humor, but keep looking around, Jen."

"Okay, here is a long box, the label says it is a steel shelf unit, assembly required. The picture on the box makes it look sturdy."

"Now that will come in handy," I said. "So would these tables and chairs I just found."

"You know what, Codi?" Jen said reflectively, "It looks like all of this stuff was ordered by a family to furnish their home."

"It does look that way," I said.

"I wonder who they are. They must be sad. It looks like a lot of planning went into this."

"Yes," I said. "They are probably a young couple like us, just starting out."

"Oh no. Now I feel really sad."

"It will be okay; I am sure they had insurance."

"Do you see anything else, Jen?"

"Just household stuff, all of which we can use."

"Okay, then, let's leave this alone until the ninety days is up. Then we can come back and take what we need. Let's go check out that 4-wheeler."

After restacking some items, we left the plane and walked through the brush to the 4-wheeler. It was a Honda, and was beat up quite badly. The key was wired to the handle bars so I un-wired it and put it in the ignition. I turned the key. Nothing. I checked for gas. There was just a tiny bit in the tank.

"Hold the brake," Jen said. "Then turn the key." I tried that. The engine did not turn over.

"Dang, Jen," this could be a nice tool for us during the summer time."

"Yes, it would be great for all types of heavy work."

"Well, I will come back with gas when I have some free time and see if I can figure out what the problem is. I am not a mechanical genius, but if the engine turns over, I can probably fix it."

We had seen enough for now and were ready to head back to the cabin. Just as we were beginning our walk toward the river, we heard a ruckus over the hill in front of the plane. Jen and I looked at each other with both surprise and anxiousness on our faces.

"What the heck," Jen said, her eyes intently locked on mine.

"No clue," I whispered my short response.

"Let's go look," Jen said daringly. Then, "Get your rifle ready first."

With shaky hands, I unshouldered my rifle and jacked a round into the chamber. With Jen close on my heels we sneaked up the hillside and stood there in the chest-high brush, looking at nothing but alder and spruce between us and the next hill. We were just about to give up our search for the noises we heard when something caught my eye far off at the base of a bigger hill.

"There!" I said, "Is that a herd of caribou?"

"Yes," Jen said. "But now look closer, down there in the trees just below us. There is a grizzly bear in the brush. Is that Pretty Girl?"

"It sure is a bear, and I think it is Pretty Girl. She is eating something."

"It looks like a caribou," Jen replied.

"Dang, that explains why she has not been hanging around the cabin. I was wondering where she was getting her food from."

Jen explained, "It is likely that this is her first caribou kill because we have not seen the herds around our area yet, so she must have been eating porcupines and other rodents before this."

"Probably berries too," I said, proudly thinking of my little bear's accomplishments.

Jen sensed my happiness over Pretty Girl's success.

"Come on proud Papa," she said, let's go home and allow her to enjoy her supper."

We exchanged satisfied smiles and then walked our way home enjoying all the wonder that surrounded us.

Chapter Nine
The Berries are Ready

The next day about noon our shipment arrived. The timing was perfect. August was upon us, and everything that needed doing was coming to a head. The berries were ripe, and would need our attention over the next couple of weeks; however, unloading the boat was the present priority. It was loaded to the gills with all of our equipment. Unloading everything went well, and was made easier because the bow of the boat had a swing down hydraulic gate that worked like a ramp when it was lowered and butted up against the shore. We laid all of the lift and ramp materials up against the bank. I started each snow machine and drove them off the boat and to the top of the bank. I would put them under the shed later. As long as I could get traction, I could drive them because they were liquid cooled engines and would not overheat in the warm weather. The boat operator, Bryce, helped me carry the generator and the winch to the site that I would put in my anchor pole for the winch system. After that, Bryce did a double check to make sure I had everything that was shipped, and he was off. I examined the pile of materials and knew my days would be filled with work for at least two weeks to come. Because of all the work I had to do, and because it was mostly a one-person job, Jen decided that she would do all the berry picking and canning on her own.

The rest of the day was spent getting tools and equipment ready for tomorrow's work. Just like we planned, I got all of the projects done around the cabin and Jen picked and canned one hundred quarts of berries. All of this took about two weeks, but the dock system was in and the boat would be safe from high water and ice. When we finally had time to stop and breathe it was August fifteenth. The days were much shorter than we were accustomed to. The sun was rising at about five thirty and setting right around ten o'clock.

It was time to think about traps and trap line trails. We had some brushing to do to make sure our trails were easily seen after the snow fell. After a few snowfalls and a couple of times running the machines down them there would be no problem unless we received a huge snowfall or experienced blizzard conditions, which could shut the trap line down.

After a few days of rest and doing some inside chores like installing the woodstove and the shower, our cabin home was pretty much complete. As always, there is work that can be done, but the essential list of must do work had everything crossed off. That felt good.

One morning right after breakfast I went outside and dumped all the traps out onto a huge pile just under the eaves of the woodshed. My plan was to run some two by fours from pole to pole on the side of the shed to use as a trap hanger. After I had the hanger made, I sat down and began the long process of checking and adjusting trap pans and tension as needed. This was a slow process, but it was one I learned from Alvin and Bill. They enjoyed it and so did I.

As I worked my mind drifted to the memories of my two friends. What a treat it would be to have them sitting here with me pointing out my rookie mistakes or just laughing at stories that were being told. The work went fast. Getting lost in memories is a great way to pass the time. When I finished, I admired the traps; they looked so nice hanging in their new spot, all separated according to size. After patting myself on the back for a job well done, I grabbed a gas can, an axe, my backpack, and my rifle. I was going to check out the 4-wheeler up by the crashed airplane. I took the backpack and axe to strip bark off of some alders so the backpack upon return would be filled with that bark and would serve as my trap dye. Dyeing and waxing the traps would take an entire day but was essential to the proper care and fast action of the trap.

The Honda had been sitting in the weeds for near two months and had suffered some damage from porcupines, which seemed especially interested in chewing on the seat. It had a few chunks of material missing from it. I poured the gas in and turned the key. Nothing happened. After that initial try, I remembered Jen said I had to hold the handbrake down when starting the machine. I did this. Nothing. I circled the Honda looking for anything that was out of place. I did not smell gas, so I figured that a broken line was not the issue. Not being mechanically inclined, I was pretty proud of myself when I saw that the spark plug wires were disconnected. I put them on and expected the machine to start. It did not.

I looked for the battery. *That has to be the problem*, I thought. The battery was under the seat. I found it after spending a few minutes learning how the seat came off the machine. There was the problem. One of the cable clamps on the battery was broken. It probably happened from the severe jolt of hitting the ground. Because the clamp was broke, it had popped off. I put it on the post and turned it. The clamp felt reasonably tight so I tried to start the machine. It made some clicking sounds and seemed to turn the engine ever so slightly, but did not start. I had to find a way to tighten that cable. As I looked around I noticed that the wire on the key was still attached. With a couple of twists, it was free. I doubled it over for added strength and then wrapped it around the cable head as tightly as its strength would allow. It worked. There was power to the starter. After a few seconds of turning over, and me finding the choke, it popped off and purred beautifully.

I forgot all about the original purpose of my mission as I hopped on the machine and turned it toward the beach. It was very hard to drive because the handle bars were bent and the front axle seemed to be out of whack. I pressed on as I could not resist the temptation of driving up to the cabin and seeing Jen's surprised look. She was surprised.

"So, this life was not good enough for you? You turned to thievery?" she asked, a huge smile beaming across her face.

"Yes," I said in my best law breaker voice. "The temptation was overpowering. There is no hope for me now. Care to join me for a ride and break the law with me?"

"No thanks, I don't want to be party to a crime," she said, as she approached the machine and hopped on behind me.

"Ha-ha," I said. "They will have to catch us first."

We drove to the beach and went downstream about ten feet before the four-wheeler sputtered and died.

"Dang," I said. "The fun is over."

"Oh, just when I had grown used to being a criminal," Jen said, as she got off the machine.

"Ah heck, I will figure out how to fix it tomorrow. Then we can resume our criminal activity."

Ha-ha, Jen laughed, "Hey, I thought you were going to dye and wax traps?"

"I am, but I want to work on this machine too."

"Okay, that works. Are you hungry?"

"Yes."

"Well then, let's get back home. I have moose stew and homemade bread."

"Oh boy, that sounds good. Lead the way."

"No, hold my hand, I am scared of bears."

We locked hands as we made our way back upstream.

"Speaking of bears," I said, "have you seen Pretty Girl?"

"No, not since she killed that caribou. I think she can take care of herself now," Jen said.

"I hope so." We walked home in silence.

## Chapter 10
## September Arrives

A couple of weeks passed by without us seeing any definite sign of Pretty Girl. There were bear tracks in the sand down by the river, and they looked to be her size. Other tracks, some much larger, were mixed in on some mornings when we went down to get water. I wondered if she had found her siblings, or where they simply tracks from passing bears. There really was no sure-fire way to tell the difference.

Once again, we noticed that the days were becoming noticeably shorter. By the end of September, we would be down to about eleven hours of daylight. Luckily, we had put in long hours of work over the summer months and felt good going into these last months before winter set in. We were using the stove in the kitchen every night, and on some days and nights we lit both stoves, but would only keep one burning on most nights to help preserve our wood supply.

Jen loved the new shower, and as time went by, we become masters of warming the water and using the track system to get it up and over the shower stall. Life in our cabin home was great. We had everything we needed without all the bills to keep everything running. Everything costs money, and getting set up in the wilderness is not cheap; but, when everything that is needed is bought and paid for, that is usually the end of the cost. The tradeoff was that we had to carry our water from the river, make our firewood, and hunt and preserve most of our food. This was enjoyment for us, and, on most days, kept us extremely busy. We wanted our life to be no other way.

One morning we woke up and decided to take the boat out and go upstream to explore beaver trapping areas, and to see if there were any moose lingering close by. Jen had a moose tag, but it was for December. That was fine with us because we had meat leftover from last year. Shooting a moose this early in the year would not be good for us. It would create a lot of work because most of the meat would have to be preserved by canning it. When we were in Fairbanks, Jen bought a bunch of sausage making equipment and Alice gave her some other things like a hand grinder and a manual stuffing machine. We were set, but that work would be for the winter, especially if we got snowed in and could not run the trap lines for a day or two.

We loaded the boat with only the things we needed. Those were the rifle and our lunch. I started the boat and while it was warming up, realized I had neglected one very important need. Gas.

"Dang," I said.

"What?" Jen questioned.

"We are low on gas, and not just in the boat."

"How much do we have?"

"The boat has about ten gallons in the tank, and there are about fifty gallons more in the barrels by the woodshed. I think we should change our plans and go into town and get gas and then see if Bryce can deliver more to us later on. We will need a lot of gas this winter for the two snow machines."

"Okay," Jen said. "I will run up to the cabin and get money and more clothes for us."

"Sounds good. While you do that I will get the two empty barrels on the boat. Then we will be set."

"See you in a couple minutes," Jen said as she trotted to the cabin. Just as I completed my work, Jen joined me back by the boat and after everything was situated, we motored into town. On the way we discussed how much money Jen had brought along and whether we needed to withdraw any from the bank. As always, when living in the wild, we had to consider our needs, so we made a list of other items that would be needed before winter set in.

We did not have any way to get in contact with Aunt Alice until we could find a phone to use. After all, this was an unexpected trip and we wanted to give her a heads up that we were in town and coming for a visit. We docked the boat and walked a couple of miles before we came to a convenience store. The manager was very nice and said it would be fine for us to use his phone. We made the call to Alice and she was there to pick us up within minutes. Needless to say, she was very happy to have us in her arms. It was always great to see Aunt Alice; Jen and I loved her very much.

"I hadn't expected to see you two for months," Alice said as she hugged us.

"I know," Jen said. "What a treat."

"We realized that our gas supply was extremely low. If we had not figured that out our trapping season would have been near impossible to run without the help of our snow machines."

"Okay, let's take care of business. What do you need to do?" Alice asked.

"Well, I said," let's go to Bryce's shop. If he is there, we can get everything lined up in one shot."

We piled in the car and I gave directions to Alice because she did not know where Bryce's shop was. In a few minutes we were there making a deal with Bryce to deliver gas to us within the next week. He also agreed to take his gas truck down where we were tied up and fill the two barrels on the boat, and the boat tank too.

When we returned to the boat, Bryce suggested that we let him take the barrels on his boat with the rest of our gas supply. He said it would be easier to unload at the cabin because he had a floor mounted hoist and a loading ramp. We readily agreed with him. He filled our boat and said he would see us by the end of the week. The deal was done. With this task completed, we felt ready for the winter trap line.

Saying goodbye to Aunt Alice was not easy. She wanted us to stay, but we thought it best to get back. Jen invited Alice to visit us if the boys would bring her up by boat, and if not, ride out after the snow fell and spend time with us then. She agreed that both options sounded good.

We made it home before nightfall. Tomorrow, we decided we would go up river to find more areas to trap beaver. After that, I figured, to put the boat away for the winter.

Early the next morning Jen and I were cruising slowly upstream with our eyes open for beaver sign. There was a lot of sign, most of it off small streams that met up with the river. The spots were very similar to the one I trapped right by the cabin last year. These would also be easily accessible by snow machine. I wanted Jen to run the trap line that I ran last year. This would keep her closer to home as it was important that we kept the stoves going during the long, dark winter days. If our canned goods froze, they would likely break the jars, and if it got cold enough, the tin cans with our vegetables and fruit in them could burst. This meant I would be doing most of the beaver trapping along with all of the other critters that would help round out the trap line. Jen would concentrate mainly on marten, fox, and lynx.

We cruised upriver for twenty miles or so and then decided that we had seen enough to satisfy our interests. As far as trapping was concerned it was now a waiting game. We needed cold weather and snow. Since the 4-wheeler was now in good running condition, I decided to put it to good use. When Jen and I returned to the cabin, we left the boat in the water and as we walked to the cabin, I told her I was going to grab one of the logging chains and try to pull logs back to the cabin with the four-wheeler. While we were upstream we noticed countless logs that would be relatively easy to get back to the cabin with the use of the Honda. A short while after we had returned to the cabin, I bungee corded the saw and the chain to the wheeler and took off upstream. The traveling was good because most of the time I could stay on the beach area which was mostly sand and silt with tennis ball sized rocks set in the soft earth, creating a layered path that served as my road way. The first log I found was about twenty feet long. *I should be able to pull that* I thought, *especially in low gear.* In minutes log was chained up and ready to go. A little push on the throttle and we were off. The wheeler was not a pretty sight with the front wheels bent, making the tires wobble, but it was a powerful little beast. Adding to its ugliness were the bent-up handle bars that looked like horns on a Texas steer. Despite the machine's less than attractive appearance, it seemed like it could pull just about anything. There were all kinds of power left over that may have allowed me to pull more than one log at a time. I decided to keep it simple, and by the end of the day I had ten logs pulled up near the woodshed. They were ready to be sawed and split. I decided put off the boat storage work for at least another day as the easy access to the firewood was too much to pass up. It ended up being two more days that I spent dragging wood back to the cabin. It was worth it. With all of this, along with what was stacked along the trail, and the stockpile in the shed, we were set for winter.

# Chapter 11
## Early Snow

"Jen, there is snow on the ground," I said from my sitting position on the bed.

I got up and meandered to one of the windows in our bedroom to get a better look. Jen only seemed mildly interested and stayed in bed. I went downstairs and slipped on my boots and stepped outside. If there were anyone to see me, I would have been quite the spectacle standing there in my underwear and boots. Since I was outside, there was no reason to go inside without a load of wood. I trotted to the woodshed and gathered an armload of wood for the stoves. Only about three inches of snow had fallen during the night, but it sure did spark my interest in setting some beaver traps. It was too early for that, but it sure was tempting.

The stoves had only coals remaining in them, but with a couple small pieces of kindling I had flames in no time, and a few minutes later there was heat emanating from the sides of both caste-iron stoves. The heat felt good, and I was now awake enough to realize that I needed coffee. We had fallen into the habit of filling the coffee pot the night before and leaving it sit out on the counter. I grabbed it and set the metal pot on the kitchen stove and added more logs to the fire. In just a few minutes I heard the water start to percolate. The smell of coffee was strong in the air when I yelled up the stairs for Jen to come down. She said that her stomach hurt and she felt a little nauseous.

"Okay, I will make something and bring it up."

"No, that is okay," she said. "I don't want anything yet."

"Do you want me to come up there and lay by you?"

"No, I will be fine. I will get up in a bit."

"Okay, let me know if you need anything."

"I will. Thanks."

I thought it a bit unusual that Jen did not want to get up in the morning. Often times she is the first one up brewing the coffee. I was hungry, and knew my stomach would not wait for Jen, so I whipped up a batch of pancakes and opened a can of Spam. Fried Spam was one of my favorite treats, and it always reminded me of when I first took off from my home and began my journey to Alaska. It made sense to carry Spam. It could be used in just about any way a person could think of, and as long as the seal was not broken, the contents would last forever. When my cakes were done and piled high on my plate beside the meat I went looking for the syrup. There was not enough left for my breakfast so I made a batch from the old standby recipe of brown sugar, white sugar, and water. There was one exception to the recipe, I now added molasses. It gave the syrup a deeper and more pleasurable flavor. It took a while to make the syrup so after it was done, I quickly reheated my pancakes by tossing them on the stove top for a minute. That did the trick. I devoured my food and got dressed. It was time to go outside and take my machine for a spin. I really enjoyed having a snow machine. Even though I had never ridden one before coming to Alaska, it was something I wanted and needed.

My snow machine had a pull start and an electric start. It started on the third pull. I did not want to go too far because the little bit of snow on the ground would not protect my track very well. After a minute or two of warm up time, I hopped on the seat and bolted out from under the shed taking a hard-left turn, zoomed up the hill to Pretty Girls den. She was not there. I went further up the hill and over a few more just to check things out. It was so cool to have the fresh snow as it served the purpose to allow me to cover a lot of ground in a short period of time. As it turned out, this little trip served as an early scouting trip.

There were plenty of tracks in the snow. Most of them were hare and ptarmigan, with a few fox tracks mixed in. I circled back around to the plane crash site. It looked really strange sitting there in the snow. In some weird way it seemed like it belonged there. From there I tooled down the river side all the while checking for beaver sign and dreaming of the first beaver catch of the year.

I returned to the cabin to check on Jen. I was bit worried because she never got sick. She was up and sitting by the stove when I walked in.

"How are you feeling," I asked.

"Better," Jen replied. "I don't know what it was, but I felt sick for a little while after waking up."

"Well, you are better now. Do you want some breakfast?"

"Maybe just a pancake."

"One pancake on the way."

Just after I started to fry her breakfast we heard a boat coming up river.

"I will bet that is Bryce with our gas supply."

"I think you are correct," Jen said. "Why don't you go ask if he wants breakfast before we unload the gas?"

"Sounds good."

I ran to the river and met Bryce just as he nosed up to the shore and lowered the ramp on his boat.

"How about some breakfast?" I invited.

"Sounds good. We can roll these barrels off in a few minutes time."

"That will work," I agreed, as I rolled the first barrel onto the sand.

Bryce was a master of transportation. He thought of everything. In no time we had the boat unloaded. He showed me some straps that we would use to tie the barrels to my trapping sled and then winch them up the bank. It looked like the perfect plan. I knew that getting the barrels up the bank and near the woodshed would be a chore and that the winch would be a tool that would pay for itself. The new snow would make the job a lot easier. The work went quickly. I really liked Bryce. He was like me and knew how to get things done efficiently.

With the unloading job complete, we headed for the cabin and entered just as Jen finished piling up two stacks of pancakes. Alongside each stack was a mound of fried Spam. Bryce smiled and said, "Now that is a breakfast."

It had been a couple hours since my first bite of food, so I was hungry again. We sat down and dug into our food while enjoying our visit with Bryce. It was always nice to have friendly visitors in the cabin. We invited him to ride out this winter with his family and spend some time with us. He agreed to do that.

Jen had eaten some of her breakfast and seemed to be feeling better. After I made sure she was okay, Bryce and I went back to the fuel barrels sitting on the beach. He helped me winch the first two barrels up the hill. Everything worked out great and I now knew that I could easily finish the project by myself. We spent a few minutes engaged in small talk before we said our goodbyes and Bryce was off motoring down the river toward Fairbanks. We had become friends, and that made me happy. I continued to work on the gas, and when all of the barrels were up on the bank, I rolled them one at a time onto my sled and pulled them to the shed with the 4-wheeler. The snow the night before could not have come at a better time. It was not enough to hinder the progress of the four-wheeler, yet was enough to allow the sled to slide with little friction between it and the ground. The hardest part was tipping them upright so each barrel stood on its end. They also needed to be off the ground, so I maneuvered each one onto planks that were laid out to resemble a pallet. After everything was in place, I covered all ten barrels with a tarp and weighed it down with lumber. The job was done. Our fuel supply was put away and we were set for the winter.

Chapter 12
Time Flies


We spent the next few weeks working around the cabin as well as brushing the trap line trails. Preparation for the trap line was an endless task, but one that I grew to love more each year. It was almost the end of October before we realized how much time had passed. The weather had turned quite cold in late September and stayed that way throughout the month of October. There was not much snow on the ground, only patches here and there where the sun could not reach. The days were short. We had put in some beaver sets close to the cabin and checked them on a daily basis. So far, we had sixteen beaver caught and on drying hoops scattered around the inside of the cabin.

Since we had the trap lines ready to go, it was time to think about moose hunting. We had pretty much cleaned up all of our wild meat supplies and were eating fresh hare and ptarmigan on a regular basis. The urge to eat fresh moose steaks drove our desire.

Jen had a bull tag for December, but we also had a cow tag that could be used in our hunting area. Because of the lack of snow, we decided we would go out on foot and look for a big healthy cow to harvest. The nights were well below freezing, and the days usually rose to slightly above the freezing mark, as far as we were concerned, perfect hunting weather. The wood shed proved to be much more than its intended purpose, and was a great addition to our property. It had a spot at the back that never sees sunlight; it was the perfect spot to hang moose quarters, especially if the weather warmed up.

The next morning, we were up early finalizing our plan for a day of hunting. Jen had her rifle ready to go and so did I. As always, my .22 revolver was on my hip. We both carried backpacks that held game bags, knives, a change of clothes, and survival gear. We ate a quick breakfast and were climbing the hill behind the cabin as the morning light gave the darkness a break for a few hours.

We had seen plenty of moose over the course of the summer. None of them were close to the cabin, however. It seemed the moose were more comfortable a few miles outside the area we used on a daily basis. We did see tracks in the river sand and mud quite frequently, so we knew they passed by us in the night, a time they would feel safe in the darkness.

When we reached the top of the first hill we stopped and used the binoculars to check the landscape for movement. Just as we figured, there were no moose to be seen. Navigating the backside of the hill was easy. It was mostly barren with only low growing plants to step over. The smells of the morning were pleasant. Both Jen and I commented on a weekly basis about how much we enjoyed the fresh smells of the wild land. Mornings like this were our favorite. There was the smell of cold, the smell of fermentation, and the sweet smell of decay produced by the breakdown of leaves that would eventually serve as fertilizer for the blueberry plants. All of this was made better by the sting of the frost as our inhaled breath passed our nostrils. This was the beauty that led to the wonders of winter.

We walked to the next hilltop and glassed the terrain. Nothing. We judged ourselves to be about a mile from the cabin, and decided to go another two miles and then turn back toward the river so we would come out upstream a few miles from our home. Essentially, by the time we got back to the cabin, our path would look like a giant triangle if viewed from the air. We stopped for a snack at the point where we would head back to the river. Jen made a peanut butter and blueberry jelly mixture that we spread on Pilot crackers, an Alaskan essential. This was a staple for us when we were far from the cabin getting firewood or working on trails. Of course, we always had coffee. We both enjoyed it very much and readily agreed that it was a must as part of our morning rituals. The coffee tasted ten times better when drank out in the cold. I never knew why that was.

After having a bite to eat we sat and discussed our plan if we did get a moose. The closer to the river the better it would be for us. Regardless of where we shot a moose, we could carry the parts to the river where I could pick them up with the 4-wheeler. Our plan sounded good. Now all we needed was a cow moose with no calves.

We took one last long look over the valley in front of us, and, seeing nothing that resembled a moose, began the second leg of our journey that would end by the river. We eventually found ourselves in a series of small rolling hills that were sparsely dotted with spruce trees. Some spots were thicker than others, but overall, the landscape was great for moose. At one thick clump of trees we plopped down and leaned against our packs. The sun was out and felt great on our faces. Soon, however, it would be dark, and I had a feeling, much colder. We decided to hike to the next hilltop and take a look, and if there was nothing to shoot, we would pick up our pace and head for home, waiting another day for a moose.

As soon as we broke the horizon of the small hill, Jen stopped and said, "Moose."

"Where?" I asked. "I can't see anything."

"It is in the spruce clump about half way down the hill and fifteen or so yards to the right."

"Do you see calves?" I whispered.

"No, and I don't know if it is a cow or a bull yet. Its head is hidden behind some spruce trees."

"Okay. Oh-oh, I see it now. It is a cow," my voice full of excitement. "Do you want to see her through the binoculars?"

"Sure, thanks."

Jen took the looking glasses and after a moment agreed with me that it was a cow. I could tell that she was looking along the entire span of the hillside and the valley for calves. She did not see any and neither did I. Because of the thickness of cover, we had the opportunity to move up a bit when the cow browsed her way behind a clump of trees. From this point we could see the valley much better and determined that the cow was by herself. She was a mature animal and did not look to be very old. We figured she had lost her calves at birth in the spring, or later on to wolf or bear predation. Either way she would be a fine animal to harvest and supply us with the majority of our winter meat.

"I think we should take her." Jen whispered.

"I agree," my voice shaking with anticipation.

"There is a perfect spot just to your left," I said. "You can get a good rest for the gun on that branch. Let's take our time so we do not startle her," I reminded Jen. "The wind is in our favor, so there is no way for her to catch our scent."

Jen saw where I was pointing and side-stepped to the small spruce that had obviously been severely raked by a bull moose. He must have been in a generous mood because he left one branch that was perfectly situated for Jen to rest her rifle on.

"Take a good aim," I whispered.

"I will."

Her words barely lost their sound before they were overtaken by the roar of the rifle. The cow moose kicked her hind legs so far up in the air that it looked like she was standing straight up on her front legs. That was a sure sign of a solid hit in the vital organs. The cow ran about fifty feet and stopped suddenly. There she stood stock still for about ten seconds, seemingly trying to figure out what just happened. Her rear end was facing us and we could see the blood pumping out both sides of her chest, and because of that, did not take the second shot. Finally, after what felt like eternity, the moose took a step forward and about three quick steps sideways in an attempt to catch her balance. She could not do it and keeled over in that spot. After a few more kicks, she lay still.

"Great shot, Jen," I said in a half yell that was filled with excitement.

"Thanks," she whispered in a shaky voice.

"Your hands are trembling," I said, smiling at her.

"I am super excited," she said. "This is always such a special event for me. I shot my first moose with Uncle Alvin, and this reminds me of that day."

"Sweet," was all I could say.

I gave Jen a big hug and then we just stood there for a moment taking in the situation. It felt so good to us, and because of that there were not a lot of words to be said. Finally, we came back to reality and realized that our work for the day had just begun. After some quick calculations, we figured it was under a mile to the river. That was good for us in respect to how far we would have to lug the huge quarters of meat.

We approached the downed moose with caution, and after a closer inspection determined that she was in fact, dead. One can never be too careful. Jen unpacked the knives and the game bags while I worked at getting the moose into position that would make quartering her much easier. When Jen was done she helped me splay the legs so that the cow was balanced on her stomach. I quickly made the cut from the base of her skull all the way to the tail and immediately began skinning down one side. Jen grabbed the other knife and went to work on the other side. We made a great team. In what seemed like a minute we had her skinned to the belly on each side. Jen stretched the hide out on the ground on her side so the freshly skinned meat would rest on it rather than on the ground where it would get dirty. I pushed the carcass over onto its side so we could cut off the first hindquarter and the front quarter on that side. The other side went just as smoothly as the first. Everything worked perfectly. We placed the four quarters of meat in game bags and prepared them to be packed out. I sawed off the head and then cut the neck at its base nearest the front of the rib cage. I rolled the giant rib cage over and extracted the guts. From there I took the heart and the liver and threw them in a game bag. I left the back straps and the tenderloins attached to the rib section. This would make it easier to carry out. After an hour of solid work, we were about ready to go. I did a final search, then loaded a front shoulder in Jen's pack and put a hindquarter on my back. We each had our own rifle to carry, but if we were going to make this in two trips, I had to carry more. I picked up the rib section and carried it like a sack full of feed in front of me.

We made it to the river just as it was getting dark. It had been a long and hard mile of walking while carrying such heavy loads. We laid the meat out on a log pile so it would cool properly and then after a short break to catch our breath, we headed back to the kill site. We both knew the work had to be done, so there was no discussion about it. We started back up the bank and away from the river when the first wolf howl penetrated the cold night air. Even though it was dark and we could not see the site where the rest of our meat was at, we knew the wolves were there or very close to the rest of our kill.

This was not good. We quickened our pace as we had no intentions of relinquishing our moose meat to a pack of wolves. We had nothing against them, but this was ours. They could kill their own meat when they wanted to do so. After a ten-minute brisk walk, and at times, almost a run, we were to a point where we needed to ready our rifles in case the wolves did not want to give up their new-found goods. They were definitely very close to the meat, but we thought maybe not feeding on it yet. Even though we were a quarter of a mile away, I had hoped they heard our approach and were having second thoughts about the safety of the pack and would quickly move off.

In an attempt to further warn the wolves of our presence and of our intent, we ran a good distance toward them and then up the final hill between us with guns in the ready position. We got to the top and could not see a thing. We did have headlamps, but their light shined only so far. Out of the light's reach, we could hear movement in the dark on the other side of the valley and at one time I did see a wolf on the horizon as he slinked in and out of the shadows.

"What do you think we should do?" I asked Jen.

"Well," she said, "we are too far away to keep them from the meat, so I think we need to take charge and head straight for kill site in an effort to scare them off, and if that works, build a fire and defend what is ours."

"Good idea. I think that will work."

"I hope so. We have nothing to lose."

"Okay, let's go," I whispered.

We picked our way down the slope, and as we went, could hear the wolves retreat in the darkness to what they must have considered a safe distance. It was an eerie feeling to hear twigs snap and not be able to see what snapped it. Most of the time it was noise

made by us, but because of the intenseness of the situation, our minds played games on us, intensifying the fear we had of being attacked. After a few intense moments we made it to our destination and immediately began collecting firewood. There was plenty available and we soon had a fire burning high and strong. Our intention was not to spend the night in the wilderness protecting our food, but if the wolves wanted to push the issue we were ready to do what needed doing. That is life in the wild. Jen kept on collecting smaller pieces of wood as I went further into the darkness for some larger pieces that would keep the fire burning for a long time. With the use of my headlamp I made one last scan and could see several spruce trees that were on the ground. I dragged two of them back near the fire. After that we decided that we had enough to keep us going for the night if need be.

Sunrise would not be until nine-thirty. That meant if we waited for daylight, we had a full eleven hours until we would be able to see anything lurking on the landscape. The wolves did not make a sound so we thought that maybe they left to find food that would be easier to come by. In the back of my mind, I did not believe they were gone and, therefore, decided that we would spend the night. The meat back at the river would be in jeopardy if a bear, that had not gone to its den yet, came along during the night. If all worked out, we would keep the entire moose for ourselves. If things didn't go as planned we would likely lose half of our meat supply.

Neither Jen nor I thought that the wolves meant to attack us. They were after free meat. Regardless of what the wolves might do or might not do, we had to get situated for the night. Our first order of business was to create a safe spot by the fire. I searched out several more logs, some with branches still attached to them and stacked them like a wall about fifteen feet from the flames. The trees would serve as a backdrop for us that would prevent anything from sneaking in from behind.

Against the logs we placed our packs and then in front of the packs, we piled up a huge stack of spruce bows that would serve as our bed. It was getting late and I could see that Jen was tired and seemed completely worn out. I had hit my limit also.

I asked Jen to sit by the fire while I finished up my work. After that we would sit down and have slices of moose meat cooked over the flames along with some peanut butter and jelly sandwiches. Jen sat down and rested while I prepared our meal. Supper hit the spot. We ate silently, both of us running possible scenarios through our minds about what might happen during the night. As we settled in for what we hoped was a quiet and uneventful night, I noticed that Jen was shivering. I dug in my pack and retrieved my heavy down jacket, fluffed it up, and then wrapped it around her. She lay back on the bows and within minutes fell soundly asleep. I stayed awake as long as possible and then drifted off to sleep. Other than me getting up to put more wood on the fire, the night was quiet and we slept peacefully in the cold winter air.

## Chapter 13
## It's Not Over Until it is Over

I opened my eyes and knew it was morning, but until I worked my watch out of my pocket and took a look, had no idea that it was still two hours before sunup. The skies had clouded over during the night and the temperatures had warmed. It was not warm enough to rain or warm enough that the meat would spoil, rather there was a definite feel of snow in the air. Jen was soundly sleeping so I rekindled the fire to make sure she stayed warm and comfortable. I kept the noise to a minimum so that she could sleep as long as she needed. We had enough water left in our flasks to last the day so I took enough out for two cups of coffee and put it in our little stainless pot to boil. After the coffee was added, the aroma spread in the early morning light and Jen began to stir.

"How are you feeling this morning, moose slayer?"

"Good. How are you?"

"I am fine. Are you ready for some coffee?"

"Yes," she replied as she sat up on the bows still wrapped comfortably in my big goose down jacket.

I poured some coffee in her tin cup and then some in mine. We let the grounds settle before we ventured the first sip.

"Ah, that tastes good."

"Yes, it does," I said, "and it always seems better over an open flame." Then went on to say, "I know this will be our third meal of pilot crackers with peanut butter and jelly, but are you interested?"

"Yes, I am," Jen said without hesitation.

While I made sandwiches, we discussed how we should go about our day. We figured it would be best to simply load the remaining quarters of meat in our packs and carry them out. So right after breakfast, I fastened the quarters to our packs and helped Jen to shoulder hers. My load was propped up on the log pile behind the fire, so all I had to do was back up to it and get the straps securely placed on my shoulders. I finished adjusting my pack after lifting it from the log. With our guns in hand, we were ready for the trek to the river. The walk seemed like it would be easier after a good night's sleep for each of us. We took our time feeling no need to rush with the full day ahead of us.

Jen took the lead and after going only about one hundred yards, she came to a sudden stop, so sudden that I ran into her pack. "There is something in that spruce clump," she said, just as we crested the first hill on our way to the river.

"I see it. That is a wolf, a big wolf."

"He is looking right at us," Jen said in a shaky voice.

"Yes, he is, and I think he means business."

"What should we do?"

Jen barely got the words out of her mouth when the huge Lobo took off at a full run straight at us. "Get behind me," I shouted to Jen. The wolf was closing the distance fast and seemed to be intent on killing us if he got the chance. At twenty-five yards I fired a shot from my 30-06 that went straight into the animal's chest. He rolled once head over behind and slid to a stop only a few feet in front of us. He kicked a few times and then lay still. Only then did I lower my rifle. A growling noise made me look toward Jen just as she pulled the trigger on a wolf sneaking up from behind. "I did not want to shoot her," Jen said, "but she kept coming."

"You did the right thing. She was working with the one I shot. If we did not have our rifles, we would be supper for them right now. Keep your eyes peeled. There has to be more out there."

"There are," Jen said. "I saw some to our right. I think they are young ones from this spring."

All was quiet for the moment. We scanned the immediate area for any sign of the other wolves, and finally located them. They had retreated far off to a hillside to our right. There were three of them, and as I figured were pups from the spring. This did not mean they were not dangerous, but without their leaders the likelihood of another attack was unlikely. We watched them for a few minutes, then decided we had to get a move on.

The two wolves that lay dead only feet from where we stood were huge animals. There was no doubt that they were the pack leaders, and we hoped, their deaths would be enough to dissuade the others from pursuing our meat supply. By killing the wolves, we had added unneeded work to our over-filled agenda. We had to skin the wolves and take the hides. Even though we had not looked forward to killing these animals, their hides were valuable and we could not let them go to waste. Jen was noticeably shaken and tired so I did the skinning by myself. After a couple of hours, we were back on the trail toward the river. We arrived with little over an hour of daylight left. We had to push forward to get home before dark. Once we cleared the brush on the river bank we could clearly see what had happened during the night. To our disappointment we saw that the wolves had found our meat where we left it. It was all gone. The bones were licked clean. Either it was an extension of the pack we had encountered, or this was a pack that had migrated to the scent of fresh meat. Either way, we had been robbed.

Our frustration and anger had reached its pinnacles because of the loss, but as we rationalized the situation it became clear that the wolves had done nothing wrong. They were following their instincts, and those instincts led them to food, easily attainable food. We could not argue that. Wolves are wolves, they do what wolves do. We still had a half of a moose strapped to our backs. Rather than leave it on the log pile while we went to get the four-wheeler, we decided to carry it home. It started to snow on the way to the cabin, and by the time the meat was hung in the woodshed, there was an inch of fresh white on the ground. I grabbed the wolf hides and went in the cabin to prepare them for drying. It was good to be home.

# Chapter 14
## Winter Sets In

The wind picked up during the night and from our bedroom window we watched the snow swish and swirl around the cabin. Everything we needed was here in our little cabin home, so we were safe and content. I went down stairs and stoked up both fires. Both stoves were near burned out because we had slept hard from all the activity the day before and no one got up to feed the fire during the night. I went back upstairs to check on Jen. She had fallen asleep again. It was a bit alarming to me that she seemed to sleep a lot more than she used to. I lay down next to her, wrapped my arms around her shoulders, and dreamed of the trap line. I figured that when the wind and snow let up, I would pack our trails by traveling over them several times with the snow machine, and then come back to load the sleds and start the marten trapping season.

The thoughts of activities and the work that would come in the days ahead prevented me from falling asleep again. The wolf hides were a nice addition to the beaver pelts we had caught earlier in the month. There would be many more beavers to catch this year. With the help of the boat we were privileged to go further upstream with less of a time commitment. That scouting time would pay off for us this season. We had located dozens of beaver huts and knew that there were boat loads of beaver in this area. In my mind I kept hearing the voices of my dear old friends, Bill and Alvin, teaching me the skills I needed to trap and hunt in this wild land. I wished for them to be here, but knew that could never happen. Their experience and knowledge would live with me for the rest of my life. I was grateful for that.

At some point, I fell asleep. When I woke up, Jen was lying next to me with a big smile on her face.

"Good morning," she said, beaming a smile for the world to see.

"Good morning. What has you so smiley this morning?"

"Oh, I don't know. It might be the fresh snow, or it might be something else."

"Really." I said playfully, yet sarcastically. "That narrows it down."

"Well," she said. "The snow has stopped, and if you would like to, we could go up to the crash site and get the baby crib and the highchair."

"What for, we do not have room to keep it inside if we are not using it. Wait, what are you saying?"

"I am pregnant."

"What?"

"Pregnant?"

"How? Well, not how, but…"

"It was bound to happen, Codi."

"Oh boy, this is cool. Do we have to go see the doctor? Should I go get one?"

"No, silly, not yet. I think I am two months along. We will have to go soon, but can probably wait until freeze up."

"Awesome. I think about fatherhood quite often and want to be a much better father than my dad was."

"You will be. I married you for your good qualities, to include your dashing good looks."

I blushed at the compliment. We spent a couple hours lying in bed talking about our future. It felt so good to relax and envision our life out here with a child. We agreed it would be a lot of hard work and that there were plenty of dangers to look out for. Our confidence was high.

After our discussion we went down stairs for a late breakfast. Pancakes and syrup were all I needed to fuel me up for what remained of the day. There was so much work to be done and there was enough time for me to get some of it done. I looked outside and saw that the snow had slowed its pace and the wind died down, so I jumped on my machine and went to dig out the baby items from the plane. The snow was quite heavy and wet. It seemed that at least a foot had fallen, and because it was still coming down, I figured we would have perfect conditions for running the trap lines.

After I dropped off the baby items for Jen, and retrieved some tools for her so she could assembly the items, I departed to pack the trails. Traveling on the fresh snow was great. I did Jen's trails first and as I was doing so, noticed plenty of fresh marten tracks that were made sometime earlier in the day. They were partially covered in snow, but clear enough to identify. This was exciting to see. Jen would be anxious to get out here and get her traps set. Tomorrow would be the day. I made several rounds on her trail and had the whole thing packed down neatly. A nice base was incredibly important as it allowed us to have a solid trail, thus reducing the possibility of getting stuck after the snow got deep.

Daylight was fading fast, so I shot home and filled the machine with gas, popped my head in the door and kissed my wife, and then zoomed up and over the hill toward my trap line trail. I only did one pass on my route. Essentially, it started right out our front door and ended there too, one big oblong circle. Because all of the beaver sets would be along the river, I would run the inland part of the trap line first. That way I would not have to pack and carry heavy, wet beaver carcasses along the entire line.

It was well after dark when I returned home. While I was gone Jen loaded her sled and had a tarp over the top of everything so that snow dust would not cover her traps and other gear as she traveled. Besides making supper, she found time to lay out all of the items I would need in my pack. That really helped me. As far as traps and my equipment, my sled was loaded and ready, waiting for me out in the woodshed. All I had to do was hook the sled to my snow machine and hit the trail. After we ate a supper of fresh moose steaks with wild rice and gravy, accompanied by fresh bread and canned corn, I began packing all the things Jen laid out for me. I never left home without several options for starting fires, and never left without my down jacket and thermal underwear. Everything needed for me was here, and now was packed up and ready to go. All the while I worked I was smiling because I knew I had the best wife in the whole world.

"Thank you, sweetheart," I said from the middle of the room.

"You are welcome, papa," she teased from her spot at the kitchen table.

"Are you ready to catch some fur, Prego?"

"Ha-ha...nice nickname, and, yes, I am ready."

"Cool, I think you can easily set twenty marten traps and a few fox traps. Also, there should be a lynx or two for you to catch."

"Yes, yes, and yes...I am excited for the adventure of running my own line."

"Sweet, and some day when the weather is nice we should run our lines together."

"That would be great," Jen said. "Then I can give you some pointers."

"Ha-ha, I will take all the help I can get."

We finished up our final chores for the night. Jen went upstairs to light the lantern while I stoked up the stoves and snuffed out the downstairs lights. Our plan was to be at the head of our trap lines when it was light enough to see. I set the alarm for seven and wound the clock spring tight. Getting up at seven would give us plenty of time to do final preparations before hitting the trail. I turned the lantern off and hopped into bed. Jen slid into my arms and when the alarm jingled us awake, she was still there.

## Chapter 15
## Could This Be a Bumper Year

I jumped out of bed and pushed the button in to shut off the alarm. "Let's get rolling, Jen," I said from the head of the stairs just as I began descending to the kitchen.

"I will be right there. Would you get the coffee on the stove and a pan of water so I can make tea?"

"I certainly will. See you downstairs."

The stoves needed attention. It was chilly in the cabin because, unlike my usual routine, I did not wake up the last two nights. That meant the stoves were completely empty. We had accumulated a huge pile of dry kindling wood which I had split down to sizes about like a pencil, so starting a fire was as easy as throwing wood in the firebox and holding a match to it for a minute. The dampers on the stoves were wide open and after a few minutes the flames were growing and throwing heat. I chucked in larger logs that would burn for most of the morning. After about ten minutes the coffee was percolating and shortly after that Jen's water was boiling. By the time she got downstairs I had her tea bags floating in her favorite mug.

"I filled the pan with enough water for your Thermos. Do you want that filled with tea?"

"Yes, please."

"I will throw in four bags and fill it about three-quarters of the way and add sugar and lemon juice. Does that sound good?"

"Sounds great, thank you."

The night before I had remembered to saw off a big chunk of moose quarter and let it thaw on the table. As Jen sipped her tea, and between sips of my hot coffee, I cut nice steaks and fried them over the woodstove. We had leftover pancake batter so when the steaks were done, I added batter to the pan and made a few cakes. When we finished breakfast, Jen made sandwiches while I headed outside to start the machines and hook up the sleds. The skies were just beginning to lighten up as Jen came out fully prepared to run her line. I gave her a kiss and wished her good luck. She wished me the same. And, just like that, our marten season began.

I rode away from the river and to the left while Jen rode away from the river and to the right. I stopped atop the first hill and waited for better light. My goal this year was to trap a lot more fox. I spent a great deal of time reading about how to do this, and in some ways felt very knowledgeable on the subject, after all, I did catch some last year. It was not uncommon for us to see fox trotting on the hillsides and along the river. After more light graced the landscape I started my machine and drove slowly down the hillside. At the bottom there was a nice flat spot. I veered off my trail a bit and packed the snow down. Fox like to travel on trails, especially in deep snow. After today I would not drive on this little loop I had created because there would be a trap set there. I would bait it too in an effort to draw the fox in that direction. Because food was becoming increasingly hard to come by, a fox would find my slightly tainted hare and ptarmigan guts to be a very alluring scent to track down.

I un-tarped my sled and pulled my trapping bucket from its place. There was already a number two double coil spring in the pail along with a jar of the tasty innards. There was one trap placement spot that was very appealing to me. It was on the outside of the trail where the back of the snow machine ski had made its own path because of the sharp turn I made. With my trowel, I dug out a trap bed and packed the snow at the bottom down hard and added more snow until the trap would set just a little bit under grade. Fox like to step in low spots. I set the trap with gloved hands to keep the trap scent free, and then placed a small wad of sheep's wool under the pan to prevent snow from going under it when it came time to backfill with snow to cover the trap. Before placing the trap in the bed, I put down a pre-cut piece of wax paper that was an inch bigger on all sides than the trap, set the trap in place, and covered it with another piece of wax paper. After this, a thin layer of sifted snow made it look like nothing was there. I snapped the chain link onto a three-pronged drag and buried that off to one side. Out in front of the trap, and off the trail a few inches, I buried a gob of tainted guts in a hole I had dug in the snow just a few inches away from the trap, and up against a small bush growing there. With a quick squirt of fox urine on a nearby branch, the set was ready to catch a fox. I moved away from it and admired my work. With a little luck there would be a beautiful, prime red fox waiting for me the next morning. I hopped on my machine and looked for more places to make fox sets.

Before I arrived at the dense grove of spruce trees that would hold most of my marten sets, I had made four fox sets in the snow. It was almost a two mile stretch so it was not overloaded by any means. The spruce trees loomed in front of me like a black painted wall. From way out in the valley I could clearly see my trail because it looked like a tunnel going into the trees. I made the first marten set about ten yards inside the thick trees. Like most of my marten sets, it was simple. A trapper did not have to conceal the trap in order to catch these animals. They had no fear of steel unless they were caught once and got free. That would likely stick in their minds and keep them from freely working a set and being caught. Above the trap, I pounded a nail about halfway into the trunk. This would serve as a place to hang bait. I had everything from squirrels to chunks of beaver to lure them in with. At the base of the tree I usually placed a urine-based scent or a gland lure. Many times, just to shake things up, I would use a mink lure or a raccoon lure. They all seemed to work. By the time I was to the north end of the trees I had thirty-one sets made and it was dark.

I started my machine and drove toward the river. My intention was to set more fox traps on the way, but time was running short. I still had beaver sets to make. Since we had pulled the sets in after our initial catches, there were no traps to check. In a last-minute decision, I decided to head straight home to see how Jen's day had gone. The cabin lights were lit and that relieved my mind. Jen was very capable in all aspects of living in the wild, heck, she knew more than I did. That did not lessen my worries of her being alone on the trap line.

I pulled up close to the cabin and noticed a huge male lynx lying just outside the cabin door. I was impressed. Inside, Jen was cooking supper and had both stoves fully stoked. The warmth felt good to say the least.

"How was your day," she asked from her spot by the stove.

"Excellent, and yours looks like it was better than that. How did you come about harvesting that beautiful cat?"

"He was on the trail about halfway through my line. He ran ahead of me and then cut off the trail. I thought he was gone, but got the .22 ready just in case."

"Sweet," I said. "Then what?"

"Well, actually I forgot about him while I made a set and then packed my gear back in the sled. As soon as I started the engine, I saw him run uphill from the trail. He must have been sitting where I could not see him. After I pulled forward to where I had last seen him, there he was again just ahead of me. He sat there like he didn't have a care in the world."

"Is that where you shot him?"

"Yes, he fell right there, never kicked a leg."

"Nice work. He is huge. I will skin him for you after we eat supper."

"That would be great. Thank you. Now cleanup for supper. I made chili."

"Dang, that sounds good. I am starving."

I washed up in the basin of water heating on the stove in the addition. Supper was about as good it gets. Jen was such a wonderful cook.

After supper, I grabbed the lynx and took him to the woodshed where I hung him from a skinning gambrel that was mounted in there. The cat was only partially frozen, so the process was quite easy. His fur was thick and luxurious and would demand top dollar at any fur sale. Before going back to the cabin to stretch the hide, I cut the cat carcass into six pieces and threw them in a bucket for use on the trap line. The big tom stretched the full length of the stretcher board. Jen was very proud of her catch and beamed at it as I hung the drying board from nails driven into the rafters.

"You did a nice job skinning him," she commented.

"Thanks, it was fun. Every time I skin something, my speed with the knife increases and my mistakes are fewer."

"Yes, I noticed it did not take you very long to pull the hide from the carcass."

I changed the subject from the lynx because I realized we did not talk about the number of sets that each of us put out. "I made thirty-one marten sets and a handful of fox sets. There is a lot of sign."

"I noticed that too," Jen said. "I made twenty marten sets, but have a few spots for fox and lynx that I plan on setting tomorrow."

"Excellent, your day will be pretty quick then."

"Yes, that is what I hope for."

"Well," I said, "My day will be long. I will leave before daylight and get most of my traps checked before sun up. That way, I can make a bunch of beaver sets before dark since I ran out of time to make them today."

"That sounds like a good plan. I will have supper ready when you get here."

"Good. By the way, when do you want to see the doctor?"

"I think as soon as the river freezes better. The ice does not look good enough yet."

"Yes, I saw that. Hopefully it will freeze solid in the next few days."

"There is not a big rush, after all, I feel great." Jen said, "But do get tired more easily than normal."

"I noticed that, but it is to be expected, I would think."

"If the weather stays cold," Jen said, "let's plan on going in two weeks."

"Okay, that sounds good to me."

After our discussion ended we did a little work around the cabin before going to bed. I made sandwiches and filled my water jug. The coffee pot was topped and waiting on the table. My plan was to be on my way within a half hour of waking up.

The alarm rattled as its call shook me from a deep sleep. The bed was warm and comfortable, but my trapping fever was on high. I got up and shut off the alarm and asked Jen if she wanted it reset. She said no. Downstairs, I set the coffee on the stove and stoked both fires. After dressing for the day, I went outside and fired up my machine and filled it with gas. Jen's machine needed gas, so I topped that off. Everything looked good with sled and machine so I shut it off and went inside to get what was needed. Most of the coffee went in the Thermos, but I did get a few sips down from my mug before anticipation overtook me and I hit the trail.

As soon as my headlight hit the area of the first set, I could see it was tore up, but could not see any animal. The trap was on a drag, so I would have to follow the drag marks and hopefully have a prime fox there for me. I shut off the engine and the noise of the machine died. Immediately I could hear rustling off in the dark. I walked that direction and soon my headlamp caught the movements of a fox bouncing beneath a spruce tree. The three-pronged drag was caught on a low hanging branch from another tree. The fox heard my approach and by the time I got to him he was in the fighting position, looking in my direction and snarling. I quickly dispatched the animal with a well-placed shot from my .22, and hung him by the back foot from a tree branch. Bill taught me to always carry a length of rope with me for this purpose. While remaking the set, the fox would bleed out and it would reduce the mess in the sled, thus keeping the fur as clean as possible. The fox was a large male and had a beautiful mane that fluffed up and framed his face. It was a good fox to catch and would demand top dollar at the spring fur sale.

I remade the set in its original spot because the trap bed was not tore-up at all. The big fox had made quick work making it to the trees where he got tangled. With a little added scent, the set was complete. I trekked back to the fox and untied the rope carrying him carefully so he did not drag on the ground. After I put him in the sled and secured the tarp, I brushed out my tracks with a spruce bow. I liked to leave a set area looking as natural as possible. The remaining fox traps were empty, and that disappointed me a little bit, but as soon as I reached the heavy spruce grove, I saw a marten hanging from the first set. It was a female with nice fur. I was happy. The first three sets held nice catches. Then I went on a dry spell for the next ten sets, catching nothing. There was no sense stopping at those sets as there was nothing for me to do. The bait and scents used were still in place. They would produce fur in good time.

The fourteenth set was the charm. It held a huge male marten. I released him from the trap and tossed him toward the sled. Remaking the set was easy and fast. The final touch was a refreshing of the scent and lure and I was on down the trail. I ended up catching nine marten, not bad for the first day.

I was making great time, so decided to set more fox traps on my way to the river. There was plenty of sign, so there should be fur in them tomorrow. My real excitement was for beaver. We had discovered so many good spots along the river, and now the ice on the sloughs was thick enough for me to walk on. That meant I could pull my machine right next to the ice and work out of the sled. Eventually, the ice would hold my entire rig. The spot I was at this far up the river was very similar to those trapped last year with the help of Alvin and Bill. That year of experience, and the summer to think things over, really helped my efficiency. I worked hard for a few hours and made many under ice sets. Daylight was coming close to the end of its run for this day. I had one more place that needed to be set before I called it quits. I packed up my gear and headed downstream.

The last spot was a neat set up. There was a channel leading off the river that went into a small pond. The beaver were using the pond, but I was unsure what the reason was. Right next to the channel was a bank den that was surely being used as a place to feed. I set a 330-Conibear in the channel, and then, when I approached the bank den, I heard a beaver exit and saw his bubbles under the ice. The ice was thin here, and with one chop from my chisel, I was through. I made the hole big enough to accept the trap and began the process of creating the set. That is when I heard the most peculiar sound. It was a big "WOOF". If I had not turned and saw the stabilizer sticks that were holding the first set in position, I would not have solved the mystery. They were bouncing wildly in the yet unfrozen hole. I had caught a beaver while only a few steps from the trap.

My excitement peaked. Now I had a story that held the same type of clout that Jen's lynx story from yesterday enjoyed. I finished making my set, and in the meantime, the sticks stopped moving and that meant the beaver was dead. It was a strange sensation knowing that the set wasn't even in the water five minutes and already a beaver was caught. I lifted the sticks to the point where I could see the beaver tail. It was a big one. I could tell that he was old too; his tail had many fight scars with some chunks actually missing from it. The hole needed to be much bigger in order to extract the beaver. That was easily accomplished with a few well-placed strikes from my chisel. Again, I grabbed the chain and hoisted the enormous beaver onto the ice only to find out he was too big to fit completely in the trap. Because of his size, the clenched jaws of the trap rested squarely on top of his head just in front of the ears. Lucky catch, I said to myself. I had never seen such a huge creature come out of the water. Bill and Alvin had both told me stories about monster beaver they caught, and I figured this must be my prize as far as size goes.

I reset the trap but do not think my eyes left the beaver during that process. It was an absolute monster. I was actually laughing to myself. It looked like a black bear laying on the ice. When its fur was dry, it would be a beautiful brownish orange color, but now in the fading light and with its wet fur, the animal looked pure black. I heaved the huge beaver into the sled next to the rest of the day's catch and turned toward home. It had been a great day for me on the trap line. I was pumped. I hoped Jen had the same type of day.

Again, the cabin was lit up and Jen was working at the table when I walked in.

"Hey hon," I said. "How was your day?"

"Good, I caught seven marten."

"Sweet," I said. "I caught nine marten and one fox. Oh yes, and one enormous beaver."

"Ha-ha, are you trying to trump my trap line feats? If I remember correctly, you did not have beaver traps set yet."

"I didn't, but then I did. Come outside and I will show you and then tell the story."

We walked out the door and Jen started laughing. "Is that really a beaver?"

"Yes."

"It looks like a bear."

"I know. That is what I thought."

"How did you catch it?"

"Well," I began my story, "I was making the second of two sets at this one spot upriver when I heard this trap go off. It sounded like a big "WOOF", something like a startled bear might make. I was startled, but when I turned I saw the stabilizer sticks bouncing around. I knew right away that it was a beaver."

"That is awesome. Were you surprised at how big the beaver was when you first saw it?"

"Yes, and I am still in awe."

"You should be. I don't think I have ever seen a beaver that big. Uncle Alvin and Bill would be proud of your accomplishment."

"Yes," I said. "I bet they would be."

"Let's eat some supper," Jen said. "We have a lot of work ahead of us."

The end of the day for us was never early. We had sixteen marten to skin and stretch, along with one fox and the beaver. Even though we were tired from the day's work, we enjoyed our nights putting up our pelts. They looked so nice hanging from the rafters drying. One thing was for sure. We had to keep up on the skinning because each day would bring in more fur, and if we got behind the work would become a chore. We were in bed by eleven filled with anticipation for the next day.

# Chapter 16
## Winter is Cruising Along

Like the morning before, I was up and ready for the trail well before sun up. If all went well today, and the ice looked safe enough, I would scoot across the river and check out the trapping situation over there. In two years of trapping, I had never seen another person out here running a line, so I felt confident that there would be plenty of opportunity across the water. My morning routine at the cabin was pretty much the same every day. Coffee and sandwiches were a must, and along with other treats that Jen made, were always packed for every trip. Trap line work was grueling, so by the time it was ten in the morning, I was terribly hungry and needed to stop and devour a couple sandwiches and half of the coffee. Time continued to fly by. It was closing in on the middle of November, so our day light was between five and six hours. That is not much time to run a line as long as mine. My plan was to always be at the first beaver set by daylight. That would be approximately quarter to ten in the morning.

To my surprise, there was a light snow falling when I went outside. Mornings like this one were magical. Over time, I never tired of being in the dark, racing down the trail while the snow was flashing in the headlights. An even bigger surprise was that I had a fox in each of my first two sets.

One was a small male, probably a kit from this year, while the other one was a nice sized female. I figured, after examining the tracks that they were traveling together. The female was in the first trap and had hung up on some brush only a few feet from the set. The small male was not hung up and made a lunge at me when I pulled close and cut the engine. I jumped off my machine so that it was between us, pulled out my .22 Smith and Wesson, and dispatched the feisty critter. When all of my work was done there, I proceeded to the trees where the marten sets began.

If there was nothing in the trap and the bait looked good, I drove by without stopping. Many times, I did not need my head lamp as the light on the snow machine lit the area up nicely. This really helped me save time. The first four traps were empty and showed no sign of being visited during the night. Finally, at the fifth set, there was a nice male in the trap. He was dead and looked beautiful hanging there with a light snow layer on his shiny pelt. About midway through this clump of spruce there was a little valley that had some alders growing in it. It was quite easy to get through with my machine and the sled. Today I noticed fresh lynx tracks in the fresh snow and decided to stop and build a cubby set and throw in some beaver meat as a bait. I reasoned that the cat would use the trail, so I made the cubby just a few feet away from my snow machine tracks. After digging through the snow to get down to the ground, I laid spruce bows over the top of what looked like a three-sided box made of snow and plugged the hole in front facing the trail with a 330-Conibear. Now the set was fully enclosed, and any animal that wanted the meat bait inside, would have to go through the trap and be caught. I anchored it with sticks driven into the hard snow. It looked good and was reasonably stable. The snow cave cubby set was done. I hoped for a big lynx to be caught and waiting for me the next morning.

It was an excellent day for marten. I collected sixteen out of thirty-one sets. With that many being caught in this small area, I would pull the traps tomorrow and then hopefully reset them the next day on the other side of the river. I was happy with my catch but was a little concerned that I had taken too many from this area. If I had time I would circle back around and pull the sets before dark. That way I would not catch any more. For now, however, I had to get moving.

Just as planned, I reached the first beaver set at daylight. The snow had stopped and the sun was out. It was warm on my parka and seemed the perfect place to enjoy my early lunch. As I was eating, I noticed the stabilizer sticks were askew at the first set. This meant there was probably a beaver waiting for me. Still, I took my time eating. There was plenty of daylight for me to accomplish all of my work and scouting for the day. The hot coffee and tasty sandwich were enough to nearly put me to sleep as I slouched back against the snow machine seat. Soon, though, the anticipation was too much to bear. I grabbed my chisel and trap pail and walked the short distance to the set.

After a few well-placed chops on the ice the hole opened up and I could see fur. Upon first look it appeared much different than beaver fur. *Could it be an otter?* I thought. That is what it was, an otter. What a sweet catch to make. Actually, I figured, there should be plenty of otter in the area. We did not see them often in the summer months, probably because we did not spend a lot of time down by the river. For some reason, however, they didn't register in my mind as an animal I would pursue with traps. This one got me interested. It was a big male and as I pulled him through the hole could see his fur was shiny and sleek. I could not wait to get him back to the cabin where I could examine him when his fur was dry.

The day ended with my second otter, another male, caught in the same trap as I caught the huge beaver in the day before. I could not believe my luck at that set. To my fox and marten catch from the morning, I added two otter and six beaver. This was a bumper of a day on the trap line. I was hopeful that Jen had made a nice catch too. If so, we would be busy all night to say the least.

The ice on the river looked good, and after cautiously walking out, chopping holes as I went, determined that it was more than enough for me to cross with the snow machine. I found a spot where the bank on the other side had a gradual incline rather than a cut bank. After giving the situation one final look, I pinned the throttle to the handle bars and scooted across the ice. It felt strange that I had never been on this side of the river. It seemed like foreign territory. I turned my machine downstream and rode the bank all the way to our cabin, checking out trapping possibilities as I went, and then shot across the river and parked in the woodshed with the sled just barely under the roof. Jen came out to greet me.

"How did you do," she asked.

"Great," I said. "How about you?"

"Six marten. I pulled all the traps."

"Good, I am going to do that tomorrow."

"So, what did you catch?"

"Sixteen marten, two fox, six beaver, and two otter."

"Seriously?" Jen questioned. "Two otter?"

"Yup, one in the first beaver set and one in the last set, the same place I caught the monster beaver yesterday."

"Excellent. We have our work cut out for us, but I know we will not be able to do all the skinning tonight, so I will finish it tomorrow while you are checking traps."

"That would be great."

"What were you doing on the other side of the river?"

"Checking for new areas to trap."

"Does it look good?"

"Yes, very good. I didn't look it over too closely, but from what I saw, it is at least as good as this side."

"Sweet. Now you have new territory. What do you say we eat supper and then get to work on the fur?"

"Supper sounds good to me."

The skinning work was tough. We worked until midnight, and surprisingly finished all of the marten and the two otters. Jen had spent most of her childhood skinning beavers with Uncle Alvin, so she was quite good at this difficult job. Her plan was to do them tomorrow and if she had time would cut up the carcass and prepare the pieces for the smokehouse. If she got that done, I would fire up our makeshift smokehouse and smoke and dry the meat. That would give us a pile of great snacks for a long time.

While we were putting up the hides, and because Jen was showing noticeably, we made plans for the trip into Fairbanks to get her in to see a doctor. Because it could take a few days to get an appointment, we decided that I would escort her to Aunt Alice's house and then return to the cabin to run the trap line and keep our home heated. We did not especially like this plan because it separated us and we both wanted to be there for her checkup. Living in the wild, however, does not offer a lot of options. Things need to be done and many times there is only one way to get the job done. This was one of those times.

Our plan would be put into motion the next day. I would go out early in the morning and pull all of my fox sets at the beginning of the trap line along with all of the marten sets. I would leave the beaver sets and the fox sets on the end of the line near the river. That way I could cross the river right in front of the cabin and travel upstream, setting traps as I went. When I reached the point where the beaver sets were, I would scoot across the river and check those traps. The line would be quite long, especially if I ventured in and away from the river to set a good-looking spot. Either way it was run, this looked to be a productive line, and it would give me time to scope out more options on that side of the river.

I added more traps to the pile already in my sled, mainly 330-Conibears and snares. My hope was that I would come across some places where there was ample wolf sign and, if I were lucky, wolverine sign. Also, my newfound interest in otter was at the top of my thinking. They were such a cool looking animal. I wanted to catch more of them if their population was as good as it seemed to be.

I kissed Jen goodbye at four the next morning, and told her I would be back in a few hours. My plans changed a bit as I thought things over before going to bed the night before. My plan now was that I would pull the traps first and then go back to the cabin and drop off any fur that was caught. This way I could unload any equipment not required for the rest of the day. I made good time on the trails. The temperature was above zero and it felt like there was snow on the way. The only catches made were two marten and three beaver. I was okay with that. If I had caught more marten, I would have been very concerned about the population for breeding purposes.

## Chapter 17
## Plans Change

As planned, I dropped everything off at the cabin, and gave a quick hello to Jen before continuing on with my day. The other side of the river was untouched trapping and hunting land. The first thing I saw after I climbed the bank directly across from the cabin was a small bull moose. I unstrapped the 30-06 from its usual spot across my chest and shoulders and immediately found the bull in the scope. Without hesitation, I pulled the trigger. The moose fell right in his tracks. My plans for the day changed quickly. I drove by the dead moose a couple of times to pack the trail down and then headed home to get Jen's machine which still had her sled attached to it. She heard me come up the trail and came outside to greet me.

"Back so soon?"

"Yes, did you hear the gunshot?"

"Yes, I did. What did you get?"

"A young bull moose. I could not pass him up."

"We need the meat, especially since we involuntarily shared half of the first moose with the wolves."

"Ha, yes, she said. This will set us up for the year."

"Do you want me to go with you?"

"No, you can finish up here, that way we can keep our plans for tomorrow."

"Okay, I will see you when you get back."

"Bye."

I jumped on Jen's machine and raced across the river. I quickly gutted the moose and then rolled him onto the sled. I planned on quartering him behind the woodshed and then hang the meat so it aged correctly. He was a nice fat animal, probably two years old. He fit nicely into the sled so I did not strap him down. Within the hour I was back at the cabin skinning him out and hanging the quarters as I sectioned them off the body. When everything was done, I hung and stretched the hide between two poles in the shed for it to dry.

It felt good to have another job out of the way. Since our life plan revolved around us growing our own food, picking berries, and hunting, this moose would save us a lot of time and money in the aisles of a grocery store. In the coming summer and spring, we planned on planting potatoes, carrots, kale, cabbage, and other cool weather crops. For the time being, however, we needed to focus on getting Jen to the hospital to see a doctor.

The next morning, just as planned we hopped on our machines and took off for Fairbanks. Before leaving, we cleaned Jen's sled and put in it only the essentials needed for the trip. Without a sled behind my machine, I would be able to make great time coming back later in the day. The ice was in great shape. We rode the edge all the way in and never saw anything to suggest that ice conditions were unsafe.

Aunt Alice was overwhelmed by our visit. She was so happy to see us that she had to sit down and catch her breath. When she recovered, she asked, "Is everything okay?"

"Yes, better than okay Auntie."

"Well, that is good to hear. Wait, what do you mean, better than okay?"

"I am going to have a baby."

"Oh yes, I had been hoping for this." She said with a huge smile and a chuckle as she jumped up and hugged us both.

"We knew you would be happy. I am over two months along. We figured we better see a doctor to make sure everything is going well."

"Oh good," said Aunt Alice. I will drive you to your appointment."

"I still need to make an appointment and hopefully stay a couple of days with you. Is that okay?"

"Yes, dear. You two take your old room."

"Codi is going back today. We have trap lines to run and the cabin has to stay heated."

"Okay," Aunt Alice said.

We finished our conversation going over the details. Jen and I decided that I should come back in three days. That would give her enough time to see the doctor and do some visiting and shopping. "Remember the bacon and eggs," I said, as I kissed her goodbye.

When I reached the cabin, it was dark. I let myself in and found the lantern and lit it. The stoves were cold, but it was not cold enough in the cabin for anything to freeze. After the fires were stoked I finished some work with the fresh hides and got them on stretchers. There were many hides that were dry and could be stacked in the rafters until we took them in for the market. I spent the rest of the night taking them off of stretchers and putting the stretchers and hides away.

I was exhausted, and it did not take me long to fall asleep. I lay awake for a few minutes; however, because the bed felt strange without Jen beside me. I woke up once during the night and filled the firebox in each stove and went back to sleep. When the alarm sounded I felt well-rested and looked forward to a long day of setting traps. After breakfast I hitched the sled to my machine and went across the river to start the new line.

I passed by the moose kill and noticed tracks there from ravens, fox, and one set that looked like a wolverine. I made two fox sets in the snow, but could not find a good place to hang a snare for a wolverine. That was okay with me. As I figured it, there would likely be a suitable place upstream for a wolverine set. The wolverine is a traveling animal. I had to find a spot that would be good for weeks to come, a set that would remain operational in all weather. As I moved along, I noticed that there seemed to be a lot more lynx activity on this side of the river. My anticipation sky-rocketed with possibilities. Several spots along the river bank showed sign where the cats were coming and going, usually walking along the ice for some distance before heading back up the bank and moving away from the water. Lynx primarily feed on the hare, but there would be no reason why they would not enjoy a meal of beaver meat.

The most intense activity was directly around beaver bank dens and the beaver lodges. Both fox and lynx spent a great deal of times in these areas; however, I never saw any sign that they made a kill. Catching a beaver in the winter would be an achievement for either animal. I made several sets where I knew there were active beaver huts. First, I made the beaver set, and then before leaving, I hung a snare on the trail coming down the bank, and in a couple cases, made snow sets right next to the underwater beaver sets. I made these sets by chipping out enough ice so that the trap rested just a little bit lower than the top of the ice. Then I put down wax paper and tucked some sheep's wool under the pan. After the trap was in its chipped-out spot, I covered it with another piece of wax paper. The reason for this was that I could fan out the snow over the trap more to make it look natural, and would prevent snow from getting under the pan, keeping the set operational. The final touch was placing a gob of lure on the dry beaver stick that anchored the beaver trap that was set below the ice. These sets looked good, and were a new thing for me. I hoped the payoff would be a few nice, big lynx.

I worked through the day and had gone well past the spot where my beaver and fox traps were set on the other side of the river. I found a spot to cross over, and then began setting traps as I headed for my existing sets, hoping for some nice fur to be waiting for me. After all of these traps were checked, I had three beaver and one fox. I pulled all of the sets. After all, I had put out forty-one sets in one day and covered about twenty miles of trail.

I was eager to get back to the cabin. Just as I was finishing up pulling traps, it began to snow. I hoped there would not be too much on the ground when I woke up the next morning. If it stayed light and fluffy it would not cause problems for my snow sets.

My night was busy preparing the new hides for the stretchers, and pulling dry hides from the stretchers and stacking them in the rafters or hanging them from a clothes line which I had tied to the back side of the stairs and stretched to one corner of the addition. It worked great. I simply clothes-pinned each hide to the line and let it hang there.

Even though our trap lines were relatively short, they produced a lot of fur. I expected that we would catch over a hundred beaver and over one hundred marten during the season. When all the other catches were factored in, and if the prices remained high, we would earn a significant income from trapping. That was a good thing since there would be another mouth to feed this year.

After all my work was done, I climbed the stairs to get ready for bed. Only then did I notice how Jen had set up a corner of our bedroom for the baby. She had the crib there and a chair she had brought in from the woodshed. It looked nice. I knew Jen had a shopping list for baby items and that soon after her return, the baby area would be fit for a prince or a princess.

I needed sleep. The next day promised to be a long day on the line, and the day after that, I had to go back to Fairbanks to pick up Jen. As I lay waiting for sleep to come, I worried a bit about leaving the traps out and not checking them for a day. That meant any animal caught in a trap would be there for up to two days. I must have fallen asleep thinking about this because when I woke up the next morning, it was still on my mind.

The idea came to me that I should snap all of the fox and lynx sets because the animals would not be killed in those traps. I would leave the otter, beaver, and marten sets in working order because those animals would be quickly dispatched in the traps. This eased my mind.

I was out the door early. As I topped the bank on the other side of the river, I saw a fox run away from the moose kill. This did not make me happy as I most likely interrupted his getting caught. When I got closer to the gut pile, movement caught my attention. It was a nice fox caught in one of the traps. This made me happy. One out of two, I thought. That is a pretty good average. After taking care of the fox and packing him in the sled, I snapped the other trap but left both of them lay in the snow. Chances were, I would remake these sets later in the week.

I did quite well on marten. By the time I was to the far end of my line, there were eight prime marten in the sled keeping company with the fox. I cut down to the river and saw that there were drag marks leading away from one of my beaver sets. Clearly, the lynx set I had made there was disturbed and the trap was gone. My eyes followed the drag marks, but I could not see anything on the other bank. I figured it dragged the trap over the hill before it got tangled in brush.

With a quick punch on the accelerator on the snow machine, I was on top of the river bank and sure enough, there was my prize, a big lynx in the crouched position snarling at me. After I killed the engine, I could hear the ferocity of his anger. His snarling and unrelenting lunges toward me rattled me a little bit. If he broke loose, I thought he might be able to take a bite out of my leg or scratch me up badly. I acted quickly, and with one well-placed shot from my .22, the cat lay dead in the snow. Since his head was downhill from his body, I left him there to bleed out while I went back and checked my beaver sets. There were four sets in this area, and my hopes were that at least one would be an otter. My hope was realized at the third set. I had placed a 330-Conibear under the ice at the opening to an abandoned beaver bank den. I had read many times that these spots are used by otter. I lucked out. As soon as I had reopened the hole above the trap, I could see the sleek fur of an otter. I slowly pulled him from the water, admiring his beauty the whole time. A moment later I had him brushed dry and was running my fingers through his plush fur. What a great addition he was to my day's catch. When all was said and done, I had two beaver, the lynx, and the otter. That is how my day ended. I went home and processed the fur and prepared to go to Fairbanks early the next morning.

I must have been tired. The alarm was not set because I thought I would get up early without it. As it was, the sky was gaining light when I rolled out of bed. It did not take me long to get ready. In fact, I did not eat breakfast, just had a quick cup of coffee and I was off. A couple hours later I was in front of Alice's house. When I opened the front door, the smell of breakfast, especially the aroma of bacon, hit me. Good choice, I thought. Jen heard me come in and came hopping down the hallway to give me a hug and a kiss. "Twins," she said."

"Who, me and you?"

"No, silly," she said smiling. In here," pointing at her belly, "twins."

"You are kidding." My smile showed some disbelief.

"Really, Codi, we are going to have twins."

"Wow! That means two. That is one more than one. We don't have two cribs."

Jen was laughing. "Not anymore. I bought another one yesterday."

I don't know why I felt so shocked at the news. I guess becoming a father gives a guy a lot to think about, and having two babies come at one time gives him more to think about.

"Are you happy?" Jen asked.

"Yes, I am. I am very happy, just a little shocked."

During breakfast Jen gave me all the news from the doctor, and Aunt Alice filled me in on the number of twins born in her family and in Alvin's family. After hearing her stories, I was no longer surprised that we would be parents of twins. It was enjoyable to hear all the stories and to find out how elated Jen was when she found out about the twins. It was afternoon by the time we got up from the table. I did not want to rush things, but we did need to get going if we were to arrive home before dark. We packed everything in Jen's sled and headed for home. Jen had made another appointment, so we would have to come back at the end of January for that checkup. Other than that, everything was good to go.

We made one last trip into the house to say goodbye to Aunt Alice. She had been listening to the radio and heard that there was a huge storm pushing across Alaska. It was coming straight out of the west and was as far north as Kotzebue and as far south as Anchorage. That meant we were right in its path and there was no way to avoid it. The good thing was that it was moving slowly and was a day or more out. We promised to see Alice in two months, and then hit the trail for home.

As we traveled west toward our cabin, we could see the storm clouds that were building hundreds of miles away. I made a mental note that I would have to fill all the open spots in the cabin with firewood, and carry a few day's supply to a spot just outside the cabin door. If the storm was as bad as the weatherman said, we would stay warm and dry for days without having to venture out to the wood shed.

As soon as we arrived at the cabin, I asked Jen if she would carry in all of our items purchased from Fairbanks into the house while I lit the fires and began moving firewood. As I worked, moving in and out of the cabin, I noticed that Jen had re-purposed the cubby hole where I had found the windows and other goodies last year. She had it lined with leftover insulation that would keep things from freezing. She bought a thermometer that she placed at the bottom by the eggs, bacon, and milk. I sat down next to her to get a closer look.

"You are incredible," I said.

She winked at me and said, "You're not bad yourself."

We had a good laugh. Now we had a natural refrigerator that would use the cold from the ground to keep our food cold, and probably be good to use year around. I went back to work, and just as I was finishing the wood hauling, Jen hoisted a five gallon bucket up from the storage refrigerator. It was filled halfway with beaver parts.

"Here is the brined beaver meat. I forgot all about it until now. Do you want to smoke it?"

"Yes, I will get the smoker ready."

"Smell it first. Is it good?"

"Yes, and very cold."

"Excellent. I will have it smoking in minutes."

My smokehouse was nothing more than a stainless steel two gallon pail and four old pallets with an old canvas thrown over the top. The can was my firebox where I would start a small fire and throw on my green or wet wood to produce smoke. It would never get hot enough to cook anything, just do a great job of curing the meat. I had a bunch of rebar that I strung from pallet to pallet that would support my old oven racks. As promised, the meat was smoking in no time at all.

I immensely enjoyed these types of things. When I looked at smokers in the store my mouth watered for one that was premade, but as time went by, I knew I could build my own and it would do as good a job or better than anything I would spend money on. All I had to do after the meat was on the racks was to roll back the tarp a couple of inches catty corner to where the fire pail was. This produced a draft and would pull the smoke across the meat before it escaped out the draft hole. It worked perfectly and best of all, I could monitor from my front door, the amount of smoke being produced. The only time I had to go add wood was when the smoke died down. I kept it going all night and only had to get up three times to stoke it.

## Chapter 18
## There is Always Danger

*December 1st*, I thought as I woke up, *it is December 1st*. After my amazement over the time of year it was and how fast everything was going, subsided, I realized that there were traps to check and there was a storm brewing. I jumped out of bed and went downstairs to stoke the fires. After quickly dressing I went out and stirred the coals in the pail and added some wet wood that I had soaking in water in a pail in the cabin. The smoke was immediate. Back inside, Jen was frying eggs and bacon. As they finished, she buttered raisin toast. That was a treat that she knew I loved but did not get much of so she bought a few loaves along with other needed supplies.

"Would you finish smoking the beaver today?" I asked.

"I sure will. Are you going to check traps with that storm on the way?"

"Yes."

"Why not wait until the storm passes? It would be safer then." Jen said with trepidation in her voice.

"I can get it all done and be back here before the weather turns bad. That way I will feel better about not having animals in any of the sets if we get snowed in for a few days."

"Promise me," Jen said, "that you will turn back the minute it starts to snow."

"I will." I could tell that Jen was very concerned and not too excited about me leaving under the circumstances, but the traps needed to be checked.

Outside, I loaded my bear hide and the moose hide that I had tanned the previous year. I hadn't been carrying them lately, but for some reason today I wanted them with me. I had been thinking a lot about Bill and Alvin lately, and these two items were as much about them as they were about me. I really missed my two old friends. Having things with me that they had held in their hands was extremely comforting to me.

Once I had everything strapped in the sled, I put more wood in the smokehouse pail and stoked both stoves in the house. Jen had a Thermos of coffee waiting and had packed a half dozen sandwiches, some candy bars, and an assortment of other goodies.

"Thank you, sweetheart," I said as I packed them in my backpack. I will come back five pounds heavier," I teased.

"Just make sure you come back," she said with a stern smile on her face.

"I will. I promise. I will see the three of you tonight." That made her smile. "I love you."

"I love you, too."

We kissed, and I was out the door.

The weather was quite warm. I crossed the river but did not stop to remake the fox sets by the moose carcass because if the storm was as bad as predicted, they would be buried in snow and not work even if an animal did come by. After I had checked all of the marten sets, there were twenty-one marten in my sled. It was a good catch. By then, the wind had picked up and the snow was coming down pretty hard. Everything else would have to wait. I promised Jen that I would turn back when it started to snow. The sky was almost black and it enveloped me faster than anything I had ever seen.

In just minutes the wind was so strong that the snowflakes looked like a wall. I could not see anything outside of ten feet. I was parked high above the river on a cut bank so all I had to do was turn around and follow the river bank all the way to the cabin. The wind was coming from straight upstream. I hoped that after I got faced downstream I would be able to see well enough to get home.

The snow machine engine popped off when I turned the key. I cranked the handle bars hard to the right and started to make my turn, but about halfway into it something did not feel right. By the time I realized what was happening I felt the machine tip over. Instantly, I knew it was too late to save myself from rolling over. Even though I could not see a thing, I knew that the left ski went over the high cut bank. In an attempt to pull out of the situation, I gunned the engine and turned even harder to the right. It was no use. I saw nothing but white. I heard nothing but crushing plastic and fiberglass. I felt nothing but pain. Over and over I went, the heavy machine battering my body with each horrifying turn. When everything stopped moving I was under some snow and trapped under the sled or the snow machine. I could not tell which one for sure. My chest hurt and it was hard to breathe. I freed one arm that was pinned behind me and felt around to finally figure out that the snow machine was sitting upright and that I was underneath the tunnel area and between the skis. I tried to lift the machine, but when I did my left arm, that was awkwardly stuffed behind my back, felt the pressure from the push and I screamed in pain.

Despite the pain, I had found a way to dig myself out. After a few minutes of grueling work, I had cleared enough snow from around me so that I could roll to my side. This freed the other arm and intensified the pain that was radiating from the bent appendage. The wind and snow howled and hissed past me as I tried to find a place to rest my aching arm. After a short rest and some thought, I tried to shimmy forward. That worked to some degree so I kept working myself upward. Eventually I created enough room for me to pull myself out of the snow and stand up. I felt my arm, thinking it had been crushed while rolling down the bank. Thankfully, I could not find anything to suggest it was broken. My thoughts were that I had badly torn the muscles directly above the elbow. If so, this would severely hinder my attempt to get out of my predicament. I found my way to the seat and turned the key to the off position. My machine had stopped running somewhere during the rollover. I hoped the engine would fire up when I needed it to. For the first time I thought about Jen and the babies and a tear escaped my eye. From that point, all I could think about was that I had really screwed up this time.

A simple trap line run had suddenly turned into a life and death situation. There was no way I could get home in a storm of this magnitude so I began to prepare for the night. Every once in a while, I would get a glimpse of the bank that I had rolled down. I had landed at the farthest out point to where the bank met the ice. If I could unhook the sled and pull it over the back of the snow machine, I would have the beginnings of a shelter. After several minutes of blind work, the sled was unhitched.

I unloaded the sled, piling up all the critters that I had caught as best I could so that they were out of the way and could be easily found after this was all over with. My backpack held my tundra sleeping bag and all other survival gear to include matches and candles. I threw this, along with my moose and bear hides in the sled. I turned the sled so the hitch was facing backward and then flipped it upside down. When I was done situating it, the back of the sled was on the rear of the snow machine. I would use the canvas cover on the inside to stuff in the areas that were open because of the wedge shape of my shelter.

The snow was coming down so fast. It made me feel better that my gear was out of the elements as much as possible. The snow was quickly building up around my little structure and some was going underneath. I reached in and pulled out the canvas and fashioned it into the open areas to stop the blowing snow from working its way under the sled. This worked out pretty well. By the time my work was done outside it was completely dark. So much snow had fallen and drifted up that my little hovel seemed to be airtight. After one final mental check for things I might need, I bent down and pulled at the tarp only disturbing as much as was needed for me to slip in. As I crawled in I pushed my bear and moose hides to the backside so they would stay as dry as possible. With the help of my headlamp for light, I was able to bulldoze snow up to the opening and scoop it out with my hands. After this I brushed as much snow off of me and then laid the skins over the ice and lit a candle. With the tarp pushed back into my entrance hole, things were pretty snug.

I was hungry and realized that I had not eaten any of the food Jen packed for me. Considering my situation, the six sandwiches and the snacks didn't look like too much food. I unpacked some of the goodies and ate supper. The coffee was warm and the sandwiches were tasty. As

I chomped away, Jen came to my mind. She would be worried because the storm most certainly was to the cabin by this time. I hoped she would not come looking for me. *Just stay at home*, I thought. *Stay at home*. I was sad. I was safe, but Jen did not know this. I was more worried for her than I was for myself because I

knew that if at all possible, she would come looking for me. Both of us stuck in the storm would mean certain tragedy.

The candle light was nice and it shared a little of its heat with my face. This made me sleepy. I carefully extracted my sleeping bag from my pack and fluffed it up and laid it beside me on the already stretched out hides. The backpack would serve as my pillow. With a bit of a struggle I removed my boots and my snow pants and placed them off to the side. I slid into my minus thirty below tundra bag and zipped it up tight. After ten minutes or so I was snuggly warm. Remarkably, even though the wind was howling outside, there was very little air movement inside my quickly made shelter. Before drifting off into a fitful sleep I thought about how my new life began, and especially of the day I met Bill and he snuck me onto the ferry. I wished for him to be with me. Then, just before sleep, I thought of Jen and whispered in the darkness, "I will make it home, I promise."

The wind was still howling when I woke up. I turned to one side and could see a tiny bit of light when I moved my pack and looked toward the track and skis. It was not much, but it was daylight. Only then did I realize I had my watch. It was eleven in the morning. I had slept for at least twelve hours.

My thoughts went directly to Jen. By now she would be extremely frightened. I could not stand the thought of her crying and worrying about whether I was alive or dead. I wasted no time pulling on my snow pants and my boots. Once my parka was on and zipped up tight I reached for my 30-06 rifle which was not to be found. In all that had happened I forgot about my rifle. The sling must have broken free during my roll down the bank. It was laying outside somewhere, but where. I really hoped I could find it. It took a few minutes of work for me to pull the canvas back from my exit hole and then to push the drifted snow away so I could crawl out. The wind and snow stung my face. It was much colder than the day before. My heart sank. There was nothing I could do to get home that would not put my life in more danger. I felt my way around to the front of the snow machine and took care of my morning business. It was not a pleasant experience bearing my skin to the frigid elements.

I had to know if the snow machine would start. If it did, I would try to get to the cabin. I turned the key and it turned over, but did not start. My hopes were deflated as quickly as the snowflakes were lost in the wind. There was nothing else I could do outside. I could hardly see the river bank only a few feet away, and standing out there made no sense so I went through the hard work of re-entering my shelter. It was warm on the inside. The snow had caught the bottom of the sled and swirled about it until the whole thing must have looked like a small igloo from the outside. I pushed the sleeping bag far to one side and then re-lit the candle and poured some coffee. It had a tiny hint of warmth left in it. I thought it was the best coffee I had ever tasted. Two sandwiches and a candy bar later, I was energized and ready to head for home. One look outside told me that nothing had changed and I would probably have to spend another night out here in the frigid cold.

I wondered what Jen was doing. *Was she crying? Was she preparing to look for me? Had she gone out the night before looking for me and was now lost in the cold?* The thought of her suffering in the elements horrified me. Regardless of what was happening, one thing I knew for sure was that when she could travel, she would be on her way. Then I realized that she was not familiar with this part of my trap line. In the end, I would have to trust that all would work out.

Laying down for hours on end in a confined area gives the mind time to recall the past. My mind drifted to my first days and weeks living up here. I had promised myself that I would live and die by the laws of the land. *But*, I thought, *that was before I met Jen and before we knew we would have children.* Those things change a person's thinking, but it does not change the power of nature. If you tease her, she will get you. I think I teased her. I made a move without knowing precisely where I was, and look where I find myself. *If I make it back alive*, I thought, *this would be a defining point in my life.*

Laying around and thinking was not the worst part of my situation. The worst thing was how slow time seemed to go. It was like watching a pan of water come to a boil. It seemed like the minutes took forever to tick off the clock. I did my best not to look at my watch. It only made matters worse when I did.

I could not get Jen out of my mind. The thought of what she was doing continued to haunt me. Not the type of worry like she forgot about me and left me to fend for myself, rather, it was the worry about how she was handling this for herself. The idea that I knew I was safe, but she did not know, rattled me to the bones because that would be torment for her. I thought that maybe the best thing to do was to get up and make a run for it. I had high banks on both sides of the river, clearly, I would know if I left the ice. If this were possible, the snow machine would have to be in working order. The hood was cracked up badly and one of the skis was bent upward quite significantly. These things would not keep it from being ridden, but if there was significant structural damage that I could not see, it might prevent me from moving the machine at all. I wished it was easy to figure out what to do. No matter what I thought about doing, it always was accompanied by a high danger level.

I pulled the canvas cover from the opening in order to take a look outside. The weather was still raging, but since I was dressed, decided that I would go outside and make a more thorough check on the condition of the machine. I found my way to the hood and opened it up. The wind instantly grabbed the hood and tore it from the hinges and tossed it off into the blinding snow. A few cuss words emanated from my lips. I was becoming extremely frustrated with the wind and the snow. There was no going after the hood, so I dropped to my knees and felt around the engine compartment. It was packed solid with snow. It felt like cement as I grabbed handful after handful in an attempt to make enough space so I could get a good look for possible damage. It was hard to see, but when I cupped my hands around my eyes and got really close I could make things out quite good. All of the parts appeared to be where they should be. The underneath seemed to be okay. At least there were no broken parts as far as I could tell by feeling around. The roll down the hill would be considered a soft roll because of the amount of snow that was on the ground. After all of this work, however, the pulled muscles in my arm hurt badly and felt as if they were erupting from my jacket sleeve.

I wanted to turn the snow machine on its side but that would mean my little hovel would be destroyed and my arm would be worse for the wear. I decided against that, and instead, tried to start the engine. Once again, it turned over, but did not start. The light had faded from the afternoon sky, and, once again, it was completely dark. After taking a long look around, in hopes of seeing a faint light shimmering through the storm, and seeing nothing, I crawled back in and prepared for another lonely night. I hoped the storm would break and tomorrow night would find me at home with Jen.

## Chapter 19
## What's That Sound?

Dark comes early in December. That fact had not bothered me to this point. Now, being all alone and having no options for escape, the feeling of being trapped enveloped me. I felt like crying but knew that would do no good. I knew Jen would be crying, not because she was weak or because she was a woman. The fact is, she was a loving and caring person who easily showed her emotions. I felt bad because it was me, the person she loved most, who was responsible for her tears.

During this bout of sadness, I must have drifted off to sleep. I woke up to the smell of smoke. My disorientation prevented me from figuring out what was going on. I began to cough as I reached for my hat and headlamp. After switching the light on, I could see smoke rising up from my bear rug where the candle had fallen over. The stink of smoldering hair is what had forced me from a deep sleep. In my mind it seemed as though I had blown out the candle, but in reality, the truth was that I had fallen asleep without doing so and had probably knocked it over.

I quickly snuffed out the smoking fur and then opened the entrance hole to help air the place out. I noticed immediately that the wind had died down considerably, and the stars were out. It was cold, noticeably colder than the day before. My watch read three in the morning. I had slept a long time. The thought came to me that I should get up and see if the snow machine would start. If it did, I would be home for breakfast. After considering everything that had gone wrong and everything that could go wrong, I decided to wait until near daylight before making a move. *That makes the most sense* I assured myself as I drifted back to sleep.

*What's that sound?* The question rumbled in my half sleeping brain. *It sounds like a snow machine. Maybe someone is coming for a visit.* My brain was telling me I was at home and someone was riding a machine in to visit with Jen and me.

I came to my senses. "No!" I screamed at the top of my lungs. "It has to be Jen! She found me!" I ripped at the canvas door plug and scrambled through the entrance hole just in time to see tail lights go around the bend. Without hesitation, I scrambled back inside and pulled on all of my cloths and quickly donned my boots. Within minutes I was back outside. I glanced at my watch. It was five o'clock am. If that was Jen, she had gotten an early start. I trudged out in the deep snow until I could see around the bend. There was a long, straight length of river with no sign of anyone. Other than the tracks made by the passing machine, it was like no one had ever been there. I rationalized that it had to be Jen. *Who else*, I thought, *would be on the river at this time*. My biggest worry was that she would not come back this way.

I made up my mind. One way or the other, I was going to be back at our cabin home that night. Whether I had to walk or whether I would be found, I was going home. The first thing I did was turn the sled upright and toss all of my sleeping gear inside. There was considerable digging to be done to find my fur, and while doing that work, I kept an ear cocked toward the river for any sound that meant someone was approaching. My next job was to turn the sled and hitch it to the snow machine. That went quite well, although my progress was less efficient with the sore arm. As much as I needed full power from my injured arm, it simply was not there. The pain was too much to handle and forced me to let go of what I was lifting or tugging at.

The snow machine was a horrible sight. By the time I completed the snow removal from the engine compartment, it was starting to get light. Every few seconds I would glance upstream in hopes of catching sight of Jen. I knew it was her out looking for me. There was absolutely no question about that.

The key turned, but the engine did not. The battery was dead. I wasted no time. My mind was made up; I was going home. Still, there was hope that it would be on the snow machine, but after ten minutes of exhaustive work on the pull start, and considerable tinkering on the engine, I gave up. I thought about looking for my rifle but soon realized it would have to wait. There was no time for that. I packed the last sandwich into the pack and headed for the trail made by Jen's machine and turned downstream following the path that would lead me home.

I walked for a few hours. It was not fun walking as the snow was soft and fluffy even after being run over by a snow machine. I took more tumbles than I cared to count. My focus was on my home and my family, nothing else, so pushed forward, forcing myself up after every fall.

Darkness came and there was no sign of help. I figured that I had walked half the distance. It was hard for me to tell because when I ran the line checking traps, I was working from the bank, making short jaunts inland to makes sets. Everything looked different from the river point of view. At least once before it got dark out, I would have sworn that I heard a snow machine pass on the side of the river that our cabin was on, but with the sun shining bright, there was no headlight for me to see. I passed it off as wishful thinking. My enthusiasm began to wane. It was blistering cold and the wind had picked up, blowing directly in my face. There was nothing to do but continue walking. I had long since eaten the last sandwich and had not had anything to drink since the coffee ran out. I was tired and my energy was all but gone. I trudged on and began to shiver. I wished for my sleeping bag so I could wrap it around me. It would definitely have helped defend me from the cold wind.

At least three times I saw headlights coming at me, but each time they fizzled into nothing but a deep snow trail in front of me. *Five miles*, I thought. *I can do that, just keep walking.* I thought of Jen and our unborn children. I saw them growing up, me watching from a tree branch. It felt so silly to me, so strange not to be in their lives. Another mile walked, and then something changed in me. I could feel it. A loss. I was losing control. As time went by I seemed to lose brain function. There was an insatiable feeling burning in me that repeatedly begged me to sit down and rest. Even though a rest was tempting to my tired body and tired mind, I did not obey the voice. Still, I knew I was getting weaker and more disorientated as the minutes went by. There was no option for me. I had to keep walking and hope for the best.

The shivering in my body increased as the imaginary headlight after headlight came and went flying past me down the trail. Then, after a long time of walking with nothing but sadness in my mind, I saw something in the distance. It was a headlight and it came with sound. *How weird that is*, I thought. *It is a hallucination, they are getting more complex.* More deflated than ever, I lowered my eyes to the snow in front of me and stopped walking. My body wanted to give up. My brain would not let it. The light bounced on the snow, making it sparkle. I watched it with little concern. *Another trick*, I thought. But, there was one difference this time. The sound was so loud, so loud that it irritated me to the point of wishing it away. I plugged my ears, and stood there for what felt like hours, the cold infiltrating my jacket and chilling my already cold skin. Finally, in a daze, I looked up. It was Jen, she was walking toward me. She was smiling at me. I hugged her. She was real.

"Sit down," she said in her beautiful, calm voice.

"Are you real?"

"Yes, silly man, I am real."

"Then kiss me and warm my face."

She kissed me. She was real. Jen kneeled in front of me and with shaking hands poured hot chocolate from her Thermos. Its steam soothing my cold nostrils and lips. It tasted better than anything I could remember.

"Just a few sips, sweetheart, and then we have to get home. You have to get warmed up fast."

"How far away?"

"Three miles, we are almost there."

Jen helped me swing my right foot over the seat and jumped on in front of me. "Hang on!" She shouted, we are going home.

## Chapter 20
## The Cabin Home

The lantern light in the cabin hurt my eyes, but the warmth of the fires burning in the stoves warmed me to the core. It felt strange to be back. Jen was hustling and bustling around the kitchen preparing everything she needed to get my body warm again. It was clear to me that she was upset, as her usual, quiet ways were replaced with the heavy setting down of pans and the agitated way of her walk. She had a right to be angry with me. Jen stripped me of my cold, wet clothes and wrapped me in a heavy, warm blanket. I was shaking more violently than before and could not drink the warm hot chocolate Jen had for me. I sat on the floor next to the stove while Jen handled the cup, raising it to my lips so I could sip hot liquid without burning myself. Slowly, over the course of a couple hours, the shakes subsided and I began to feel normal again. We had not spoken for a long time, it was for the best. Jen needed time to calm herself, and I needed time to consider what I had put her through. I searched for the best words to start a conversation, and then simply said,

"Thank you, sweetheart, for coming after me."

"You scared the crap out of me. I am so angry at you." She snapped at me.

With those words, I knew Jen was angry with me. She never spoke to me in that tone and never banged around the kitchen like that before. Suddenly, she began to cry. All of her emotions were coming out in one great avalanche of fear and frustration.

"I am sorry to put you through this mess. I thought about you and the babies constantly. I could not get home, there was no way."

Her sobbing quieted, she was realizing we were all safe. "I know, it's just that I was so frightened. I did not know where you were and whether you were alive or dead. I just did not know. That was the worst part."

"I know. I made a foolish mistake out there and it nearly cost me my life. I am sorry."

Jen moved from the chair to the floor and buried her head in my chest. We sat there for a long time talking about the last few days. Jen had left the cabin very early in the morning to search for me. She had driven right by my makeshift hut, but it was dark and to her nothing would have been visible. She went another ten miles upstream, but soon realized that was far beyond the range of my trap line so she headed down the other side of the river toward the cabin. It was her that I heard while walking on the river ice. It felt so good to me that Jen put in such great effort to find me. I wondered how many people out there had a wife as special as mine. None! That was my answer.

Before embarking on an all-out attempt to find me, Jen warmed up at the cabin and then headed back up river where she reasoned was most likely where I would be. She was prepared to go until she found me or she died. "When I first saw you," she said, "I thought it was dream."

"When I first saw you," I said with a nervous chuckle, "I thought I was hallucinating. I was so cold, and my body temperature was so low that I was starting to shut down. Before you actually drove up, I must have imagined seeing you at least ten times. It was all in my head"

"I can't get over how odd you looked standing in the dark, motionless, my headlight undulating with the lay of the uneven snow. You did not look real. It seemed like you were a tree trunk broken off six feet from the ground and somehow placed on the river ice. Very odd, very odd."

"My mind was already playing games with me, probably from hypothermia, dehydration, and fatigue."

"Well, all is well now, but we have to make some huge changes on how we do things out here."

"I agree."

"There are so many dangers and we have children on the way. They will need us constantly. Our way of life depends on the well-being of both of us. Without you, I have no life out here."

"Speaking of the babies," I said, hoping to change the subject

"I can't wait for them to be born. When exactly is the due date?"

"The doctor figures the middle of June."

"That is a good time because we will have less work to do, and to make it even easier, I will try to get all of our wood supply for next winter done this spring."

"That would really help and would also allow us to spend more time together with the babies."

"What wood I can't get back to the cabin will be stacked along the trails ready for pickup this winter."

"I like this plan," Jen said. "It should work out fine."

Our conversation dwindled. We had worked out most of our fears and frustrations and were back to our normal selves. Now that I was warm and hydrated, the hunger pains hit me. Jen made me a sandwich and poured some soup from a Thermos she had in her backpack. No sooner than the food hit my belly, I wanted sleep. I stoked both fires and we went upstairs to bed. Being home never felt so good. We slept.

## Chapter 21
## Picking up the Pieces

We slept well into the morning. By the time we rolled out of bed, the sun was as high as it would get for the day. My first thought was how nice it would be in late January and the rest of the winter because of the amount of daylight that would rapidly return. January is the month of the sun, it comes back quickly, with February and March being months of significant light gains.

We went down stairs to a more than chilly kitchen. I had stoked up once during the night, but that had long burned down, leaving only a few coals in each stove. After tossing in some dry kindling, I had the fires roaring in minutes. Jen was right behind me cracking eggs and getting bacon ready for the fry pan. She told me that I could make pancakes if I wanted them. I did. The breakfast was so good, but by the time we finished up, it was low light outside. There would be no work done today.

We took advantage of a slow day. It felt good to relax and worry about nothing. After breakfast we lounged around the stove drinking coffee and discussing how we would retrieve my snow machine, my rifle, and all of the furs. We agreed that the next day, weather permitting, we would venture out and haul back everything we could. That meant we would take Jen's snow machine with an empty sled. If my machine did not start, we would roll it on Jen's sled, tie it down, and haul it home. We might even be able to leave my sled hitched up to my machine. It all depended on the snow and how packed our trail up the river was.

The rest of the day was equally as lazy as the first part of our day. Jen's anger toward me had dissipated, and things were settled between us. We had plenty of firewood in the cabin, thanks to my stocking up before the storm. After looking around for work to do, we decided to put away some of the dry hides. The extra room created by pulling them from the stretchers and storing them in the rafters was great and made the cabin feel roomier. Just after dark, I donned my winter clothes and went outside to check Jen's machine for gas, and to put some tools and other supplies in the sled. Everything was ready for us to hit the trail in the morning.

While I was outside, Jen had fixed a plate of smoked beaver meat, herring, and canned sardines. It was a snack fit for kings and queens. The beaver was exceptional, and we had a good supply in our subterranean refrigerator. One thing was for sure, once we got caught up with recovering our equipment and getting back on the trap line, we needed to make sausage and jerky out of some of the moose meat that was still hanging in the woodshed. After that was done, we would have enough fresh meat remaining to last the winter. At some point, when the weather warmed, we would pressure can everything left when it could no longer be kept cool enough.

Because of Jen's work creating our natural refrigerator, we could store many food items year around. Our smoked sausages, jerky, and even smoked hot dogs would do perfectly well down there. Right now, we had milk, eggs, bacon, and beaver meat. The thermometer seemed to hover a bit above the freezing mark. Just to make sure the milk did not spoil, we kept several gallons frozen in a tub outside the front door.

We went to bed about eleven that evening, and planned to be on the trail before daylight. Judging by the night's weather, it would be a cold trip. Our winter weather gear would keep us warm, and the tall windshield on Jen's machine would serve as an effective windbreak.

Back into our routine, we were up early, and after an hour of drinking coffee and eating breakfast, got dressed and went outside. It was cold. The outdoor thermometer read minus thirty-seven degrees. The starter on the snow machine grunted and groaned quite a bit, the engine sputtered in the frigid cold, but finally popped off and ran smoothly. I let it warm up for a long time to make sure the entire engine compartment was warm. Jen carried our only backpack for this trip. In it she had hot soups and several sandwiches, and as always, a good pile of snack items.

We hit the trail before daylight. If we had to make two trips, which was very likely, we would get most of the work done before dark. We drove for about thirty minutes, when something caught my attention far up the river. In the moonlight I could see what appeared to be a giant snake crossing the river. I stopped the machine and said, "Look, Jen. What is that dark line across the river? Is it an ice heave?"

She looked for a minute and then said, "No, caribou, it's a herd of caribou."

"Sweet. There must be a thousand of them."

"Probably more," Jen said. "I love caribou meat. It has been my favorite my entire life."

"We can go after them tomorrow if you want. If we get one, we will pressure can more of the moose meat and keep the caribou for fresh eating."

"That would be awesome."

"Okay," I said with a wink and a smile. "We will go after them tomorrow."

I fired up the machine. We drove slowly until we passed the herd. It was surprising to me that they paid so little attention to us. We continued on and made it to my snow machine before daylight. Since we had made such good time we, decided to have some hot soup to help ward off the cold. As the darkness gave way to the light of day, it became apparent that working on my machine out here would delay our getting back at a reasonable hour. After talking about the situation for a few minutes, and weighing our options, Jen hopped on her machine and made a big loop, stopping so that her sled was directly alongside my snow machine. She pulled to within inches of it. This meant that the lifting and dragging of my machine would be easier than if it were farther away. We each grabbed a ski and pulled and dragged until both skis were over the top of the sled. We then went to the back of the machine and dragged it over and then lifted it onto the sled. In minutes we had the machine on her sled. To make our task easier, I had disconnected my sled from my machine. While Jen strapped my snow machine snuggly in place, I re-hitched the sled to the piggy-backing machine and we were almost ready to go. We made sure that the furs were in a spot where they would not be damaged from bouncing around, and then tightened the tarp down to secure everything in place.

That had gone smoother than I thought it would. We took off. Jen's machine had no problem handling the load. Once up to speed, we kept it going because starting out with the big load was the hardest part, and the last thing we needed was to blow a belt on our only running machine. The trip was slow going. As much as we had hoped that a stop was not needed, we did not make it all the way back without stopping. There were a couple times when we had to stop to adjust the load. My snow machine would shift just a little bit, and that made a huge difference on whether the sled stayed upright or it tipped over. It never tipped over on us, but it sure looked like it would. Better safe than sorry was fast becoming our motto.

The caribou herd was no longer on the river. We could see some of them on a far-off hillside and thought it would be easy to find them the next day. If we went after the caribou, our day would be long because I still had all of my marten sets out, and a bunch of beaver sets to check. That did not include the fox sets that I had to locate in the deep snow and then reset. Our plans included Jen and I doing all of this together. She told me that she did not want me out of her sight for a while. That was fine with me. It is fun to have someone to share experiences with during the day. Tomorrow she would give me a lesson on caribou hunting. I was excited.

We made it back to our cabin with no major mishaps. The first move was to get my machine off of her sled and then get the twenty-one marten and the lynx in the cabin so they could thaw. It was very likely that the marten traps would be full when we checked them. I had to get my snow machine back in running order, but before I began work on it, I carried in two moose quarters. We would grind meat as it thawed and make a couple of batches of sausage and hotdogs. There was so much work to do and we had to keep plugging away to stay on top of everything. My arm only bothered me if I lifted too much with it, especially if the weight I was lifting was not close to my body. I found ways to adjust my lifting to help the arm heal more quickly. It was working. Things were looking better in that respect.

My snow machine was another matter. The hood looked like it had been through a war. We had found the hood where it had been blown to shore and caught in some brush. I took it off the sled and placed it on a stack of wood. Most of the snow was out of the engine compartment, so I could see and work easily on the problem when I found it. The engine looked good to me, so I checked wires and they all looked good. I wished for a new battery. I tried the key again. It gives one tiny grunt of a crank and then nothing. My only option was the pull start. I choked the machine and started pulling. After ten minutes, I gave it some gas, which only seemed to make it worse. After some thought, and realizing that the machine was flooded, I remembered that Bill had once told me to hold the throttle all the way down and crank the engine. I held it down with my weak arm and began pulling on the crank. After the fourth pull the machine fired and on the fifth pull it started. I let off the gas and pushed the choke in. The machine died. Immediately, I choked the machine and pulled again. It ran. I kept my hand on the throttle to make sure it got gas, and as the machine warmed, reduced the choke. My machine was idling and it sounded pretty good.

I let it run for a long time to make sure my liquid cooling system was not damaged and to hopefully charge the battery. Since the battery was not damaged, my hope was that it would take a charge. After a good check of the machine I jumped on and hit the accelerator. I went down to the river and made a big loop and then back to the house. It seemed to run perfectly. Still, Jen and I would use her machine tomorrow to give me more time to inspect mine before taking it on a long haul.

Inside the cabin, Jen had the marten all situated so they would slowly thaw out so we could skin them. The moose hind quarters were as far away from the stoves as possible. As that meat thawed, we would cut and grind it.

"Hey Jen, do you think we can get the hides off those critters yet today? We will probably have a lot in the traps tomorrow."

"Yes, and a caribou or two, also."

"We will be busy."

Each of us went about our work completely content to be in each other's company. That is what I loved most about this life. Neither one of us needed to be told what to do. We learned from each other. In a way, Jen was a gift from Alvin, and Alvin was a gift from Bill. Their lives lived on in everything we did. There wasn't much more to do in the cabin, so I went back outside and set up the smokehouse so that we could hang sausages from the rebar. I left a couple of the oven racks in place because we would likely be making jerky at the same time. After this work was done, I grabbed a five-gallon bucket and filled it with alder chunks and covered them with snow. I put this next to the kitchen stove and added snow as it melted in the bucket. The wood chips had to be soaked because I wanted them to smoke for a long time. Hopefully the sausage would be in the smoker for 24 yours at a cold smoke. When it was done smoking, we planned to finalize the curing process by bringing it up to one hundred and sixty degrees in a hot water bath. This would be done in a kettle on the stove. With that process, the sausage would be cured properly.

It was supper time and I was hungry. Jen reheated leftover soup. We enjoyed that with peanut butter mixed with honey and then spread on pilot crackers. For desert, I gnawed on some beaver jerky. The marten carcasses were thawing and a couple were ready to be skinned. After they were skinned it was an hour or two before the next ones closest to the stove were thawed enough. By mid-night, I had them all skinned and fleshed. The hide pile was growing. Even with my mishap, it looked like this would be a great season, and if prices were as good as predicted, we would not have to touch our banked money.

We got everything cleaned up and went to bed. As I lay there thinking over the last year and a half, it became clear that I had changed in many ways. It was hard for me to even put myself in context with my old life. It seemed as if I was nothing more than an observer for the first eighteen years of my life, watching as life passed by me. I thought about my parents. I did miss them for that moment, but it passed quickly. It was not that I did not love my parents. I did love them, but not in the same way as most kids do. Sadly, there was no solid connection between us. Early in my life I sought love and togetherness from my mom and dad. It never came. I gave up trying. That would not be the case with my children. They would always know that they are loved and appreciated.

My pre-sleep thoughts changed to Bill, and I found myself smiling in the darkness. He was such a loving and caring person, who had gone through great disappointment early in his life, but if not for that, we would have never met. That meant no Alvin, and no Jen. I was completely happy with my life, with exception of the loss of my two best friends.

Like magic, Pretty Girl popped into my mind. It had been a long time since we had seen her. I had no idea where she was, but one thing was for sure, she was not in her den on the hillside. I hoped she was okay, and hoped she did not get bred. Theoretically, she could have mated, but she was still undersized for a sow grizzly bear. Spring, I hoped, would bring her back around. Sleep came and my thoughts turned to dreams.

We were up early the next morning getting ready for the hunt. Jen's anticipation was fun to witness. She really liked caribou meat and was determined to come home with fresh venison. It was decided that we would take two animals, and that Jen's primary work for the next couple of weeks was to process as much meat as we desired to put in jars, and to prep everything else for the smokehouse. In the meantime, I would be running the trap line and doing the skinning and stretching of all the hides.

It was daylight by the time we first stepped outside. We noticed simultaneously that the weather had warmed quite a bit. That did not hurt our feelings one bit. I started Jen's machine and let it warm up. We took both of our backpacks with us. One held our lunches and safety gear, and the other had all of our meat saws and knives along with other equipment, including game bags.

Our plan was to ride up the river and find the place where the caribou had crossed on the ice, and then follow their tracks until we caught up with them. Jen said that they should not be very far away from where we last spotted them because there was a lot of food under the snow. The caribou would have to work for it, but the pay-off of tea leaves and other items to browse was worth it, and would keep them fat and healthy throughout the winter. She was correct. They left a nice path for us to follow. After about three miles on the trail, we found them. They had heard us coming and trotted up and over a hill. We made our final plan while their snow dust settled from the horizon.

"That is okay," Jen whispered to me. "They will not go far."

"What should I do now?" I asked.

"We will go slowly but steadily up the hill, and when we can see over the top, we will stop."

"Should we get our guns ready here?" I asked.

"Yes, and make sure when we get off to shoot, we are side by."

"Okay. That makes sense."

For safety purposes we had to make sure that one or the other was not in the line of fire. We restarted the engines and quietly made our way up the hill. Most of the animals were out of range, but there were about twenty caribou that were within one hundred yards. We hopped off the machine and took our stances and leveled our rifles.

Shoot when you are ready," Jen said.

"Okay."

I took aim and fired. The nice-sized mature cow that I had aimed at took three steps and fell. Jen's rifle rang out and I watched a nice cow drop immediately. The other ones took off at a full run. Our task was accomplished. We stood where we were for several minutes giving thanks to nature for providing such a beautiful animal for us. Shooting an animal was serious business for Jen and me; we never took it for granted. After offering our thanks, it was time to get to work. It only took a short while for us to gut the caribou and get them in the sled. I would skin them at home and have the hides tanned. Bill had told me that there was no better sleeping surface than on caribou hides. I was going to find out.

We made good time getting home, and when we arrived, Jen took the guns in the house and cleaned them. This would likely be the last time she fired hers for a long time. I would take mine with me on the trap line so a good cleaning would be nice. On this hunt I had used my 30-30 which I had found in the floor cubby hole that now served as our refrigerator. Over the past year, I worked on it and cleaned it entirely. It turned out to be a great little rifle. Still, I hoped I would find my 30-06.

We caught up on all of our work, and eventually everything went back to a normal pace. The weather remained pretty nice throughout December and up to the middle of January. Our fur catches were phenomenal. Another huge storm hit in January and complicated the trapping experience, but after it was all said and done, I reset the line and trapped until the middle of February. We had expanded our lines from the previous year and our catch showed great results because of our hard work.

After every trap was accounted for and hanging in the woodshed, and all furs were on stretchers or already dried, we counted our hides. We had seventeen lynx, one hundred and six beaver, one hundred and ninety-one marten, thirty-six fox, nine wolves, six otter, and one mink. That was a surprise. I caught that mink in one of my beaver sets. Apparently, he was headed into a beaver den in hopes of capturing a young beaver kit for his lunch. He never made it. The 330-Conibear caught him squarely behind the ears. He never knew what hit him.

We hoped that our efforts would net us over twenty thousand dollars. Operating as a seller for the first time made me slightly anxious. We were unsure of what kind of money we would actually be paid and did not have Bill or Alvin to offer their advice. I hoped the fur buyer was a straight-laced person who would not take advantage of my inexperience.

By the end of February, the number of daylight hours had increased significantly. Sun up was about eight in the morning and sun down about six in the evening. That came out to ten hours of daylight. This allowed us a lot of time to do chores, like making firewood, which would otherwise have to be done in the summer or next winter. With children on the way, we elected to do as much as possible while the weather was good. As it turned out, there was unlimited firewood to be cut across the river. I made so many trips back and forth, that as the weather warmed, had to find different paths across because I had worn a couple areas down to gravel on the banks. I used my snow machine for this work because we thought it best that I buy a new one for next year. We would keep this one for this type of work. It would be our workhorse machine.

On one trip to get more wood, I glanced down river and saw two snow machines headed toward me. I shut my machine off and waited for them to stop in front of me. They both doffed their helmets. One young man and one young woman sat there smiling at me.

"Hello Codi," the guy said.

"Hello," I said in a questioning tone.

"Do you recognize me?" he asked.

"I think so, but do not know from where."

"I am Kyle. You and your wife saved my life."

"Kyle! How are you doing? It is good to see you."

"I am fine. This is my wife, Linda Lee."

"Hello Linda Lee! Come up to the cabin. Jen will be so excited to see you."

We hurried our machines up the bank. Jen met us at the door.

"Hey Jen, guess who?"

"Kyle. I never forget a face."

"No pain on this face anymore. Hi Jen. This is my wife, Linda Lee."

"Hello Linda Lee. Come on in. I have coffee ready and bread almost finished baking. Are you hungry?"

"Oh my," Linda Lee responded. That sounds yummy. Yes. I think we both could use something to eat."

The two women disappeared into the cabin while Kyle and I stood outside looking over all the things guys like to look at. He was impressed with the cabin addition and with the woodshed. After a time, we headed into the cabin to join Jen and Linda Lee for some coffee and bread. And, of course, to show off our fine catch of fur. While we were outside, Kyle had told me that he used to trap quite a bit, but that after he got married the trapping kind of went by the wayside. Needless to say, he was impressed to see what Jen and I had done over the course of the season. I did not realize how full our cabin was until we added two people to our living space. One thing was for sure, in the very near future we would have to bundle up all the hides and head to Fairbanks to sell our furs.

We sat down to have some lunch. Kyle asked if we ever visited the crash site.

"Yes," Jen said. "We have been there a few times. Do you think about that day often?"

"Yes, every day, many times a day."

"He has nightmares," Linda Lee said. "They are becoming less frequent as time passes, however."

"Well, that was a scary day. I still cannot believe that I saw the whole thing happen from our bedroom window."

"That's right," Jen chimed in. "Codi was standing in front of the window and could actually see the pilot trying to keep the plane from crashing."

"He worked hard at it." Kyle said. "There was nothing for me to do but wait for the impact. I was in the middle of the plane. I didn't know what to do or where to go. The one thing I did know was that we were going to crash and that I was probably going to die a fiery death."

"Dang," I said, "that would be a horrifying feeling."

"It was, trust me. My life flashed through my mind. In fact, I never stopped thinking about my family."

We had to let the concept just described by Kyle sink into our brains. Understanding imminent death is not easy to process. There was so much more we wanted to know. The whole ordeal was so bizarre, it begged for questions to be asked.

"So, Kyle," Jen asked, "how did you get out of the plane without being killed?"

"Well, as I remember it, everything was slow motion in my mind, but full speed in reality. That itself is a freaky place to be. I remember the plane smacking into the ground and bouncing like a basketball, but only two times. When it hit the ground the second time, the plane split open directly in front of me. It seemed like someone simply snapped a twig in half. The worst of it was that the back part of the plane kept sliding forward, engulfing under it, the ground and everything growing there. It was like a giant monster devouring everything in its path."

"Did you jump or fall out," Jen asked, mesmerized by the details of the story.

"I think some of both," Kyle said. "I play it over and over in my mind and cannot conclude whether I jumped or fell. I think a little of both is the best way to explain it. As I said, the tail section of the plane, where I was, was still moving across the ground. The noise it made was horrifying. It stopped abruptly and the next thing I knew you guys were standing over me. I do remember thinking that I had to jump. Somewhere during the crash, I must have stopped remembering. I really wish I could remember that last part. Because of the distance I was from the plane, I can speculate that I was thrown out, but, who knows, I could have hobbled that distance in a delirious and painful state of mind."

"Wow!" That was all Jen or I could say.

We sat in silence for a few seconds. Each person in his or her own thoughts.

Finally, Linda Lee said, "Well at least you lived through the accident. I do not know what I would have done without you."

"It was an amazing feeling," Kyle said, "to open my eyes and understand that I was alive. You just would not think it would be possible."

"What happened that forced the crash?" I asked. "I mean, I saw the pilot working the controls."

"The investigators said it was most likely an electrical problem that started a fire in the engines and that must have affected the electronics. The transport company had no idea where we had crashed, but since we were off the radar, they knew the situation was bad."

"How did they find out you crashed out here?" Jen asked.

Apparently, there was a pilot in a small aircraft who was watching us, but could not help. He gave the authorities our coordinates."

"Were the two men who died your friends?"

"No, this was my first assignment with them."

"Oh yeah," I remembered. "You told us that when Jen was bandaging you up."

"Would you take us to the crash site? Linda Lee wants to see what the place looks like."

"Sure, we can go now if you are ready."

We dressed and went outside. Jen and I rode up on her machine and our guests each took their own. When we got there, Kyle seemed to be in awe of the sight. "Wow, this is the first time I am seeing this. Unreal, absolutely unreal.

Linda Lee was sobbing. Jen put her arm around her and they talked softly.

"I had no idea," Linda Lee said. "It is so hard to create a picture in your head, but when you do, and then see the actual site, the reality is much worse."

"I know," Jen responded. "Even though we have come here several times, it still seems impossible that this could have happened right out our front door."

"Kyle," his wife said. "Let's go. I have seen enough."

"Okay, I have seen all I need to."

"Will you guys spend the night?" Jen asked. "We would love your company."

"Yes," I chimed in. "It would be great to spend time with you guys."

"Do you have room for us?"

Yes, more than enough if you don't mind marten pelts hanging a few feet above your heads while you sleep."

"That is okay with me," said Linda Lee.

"And me too," replied Kyle.

"Then it is settled," Jen concluded. "Let's head to the cabin."

Since the weather was relatively warm, and the outlook for the week, according to Kyle, was supposed to be warm and pleasant, we decided to ride in the following day with Kyle and Linda Lee to sell our pelts and buy a new snow machine for me. We felt it would be safe to spend the night in Fairbanks since the weather was supposed to only dip a few degrees below freezing at night. It presented the perfect set up for us to go in to town.

Kyle helped me for the rest of the day. We bundled all of the hides and carried them to Jen's sled and secured them in place for the trip. We still had two hind quarters of caribou hanging in the shed. We gave one to our new friends. They were elated. When we finished all of our work, the ladies had treats waiting for us. There on the table was a tasty assortment of smoked beaver, smoked summer sausage, and hotdogs. With fresh bread and pilot crackers, there was nothing to want for.

The cabin seemed huge with all the furs gone. "Ha," I joked, "now you guys don't have to sleep with dead marten staring down at you."

They both laughed and remarked that either way worked for them. "We have a big home in town, but to tell you the truth," Kyle said, "I think we would both be happy in a place like this."

"I would be." Linda Lee agreed.

Before we went to bed for the night, we explained all the things that needed doing on a daily basis just to keep the home fire burning. As I found out, there are many difficulties that come with this life style, especially if one jumps in with both feet and very little experience as I did. If Kyle and Linda Lee were going to live like we live, they needed to know more before deciding. To further help her understand the amount of work that had to be done on a homestead, Jen told Linda Lee that she made at least fifty pounds of sausage and twenty-five pounds or more of hotdogs, plus all the jerky and canned caribou and moose meat. This work had to be repeated each year, as what you put away for winter food, would eventually be consumed. It was an unending process, one that we loved. All in all, we explained, we were set for meat and fish, but it came only after a lot of hard work.

It had been a long day. We all slept soundly. Only once did I get up to stoke the stoves.

# Chapter 22
## A Visit to the City

Not only did we have to get to Fairbanks to sell the furs and buy a new snow machine, we also wanted to spend time with Aunt Alice. During our time there, Jen would have to make an appointment to see a doctor and then actually visit the doctor for a checkup. Our agenda was full.

We left about ten in the morning. We were experiencing about eleven hours of daylight now, after all it was the first week of March. The days were long and that was a treat for us after the long winter months. It was a beautiful morning, a great day to travel so we took our time, enjoying all the wonders of late winter. When we finally arrived in town, we went straight to Aunt Alice's house. She was ecstatic when she saw us. Her response of total surprise was the best feature for not having communication devices. We knew that we were always welcome with Alice, so making prior arrangements was not needed or expected. Kyle and Linda Lee had turned off and headed for their house just as we entered Fairbanks. They promised to visit again.

After our greeting with Alice was done and we had time to sit and talk about everything that had happened over the winter, Jen made some phone calls and set up her doctor appointment. I got on the phone right after she was done and set up a time to visit the fur dealer and then made a call to the snow machine dealer to have him set up my new machine for me. I ordered the same machine, only one year newer. The next day, Jen and Alice would drop me off at the fur shop and then go about their business along with doing some visiting with close relatives. I would walk wherever I needed to go. Fairbanks is not a big city and most places can be assessed quite easily on foot. I could always take a cab if need be.

After breakfast the next day we put our plan into action. Jen and Alice helped me carry the hides in at the fur dealer's place. I knew, from doing some reading the night before, that some trappers would not be selling their furs because some of the prices were disappointing, especially otter and beaver. Their market had taken a huge drop because the fur coat industry was at a significant low. We did not have the luxury of keeping our fur another year. First off, storing it would be a problem, and there was always the worry of pests ruining the hides over the summer. If we were to make our lives from what we earned from the land, we would have to accept the market where it was.

I could tell right away that the buyer knew I was a relative rookie, but I stood my ground during our negotiations over the prices he offered. I did not have a leg to stand on with the beaver. With the marten, however, he tried to get them for forty dollars each. That was close to half of their value. After some back and forth, he came around and gave a seventy-dollar average. I really despised the idea of the fur dealer trying to rip me off. It was clearly an attempt to low ball me to make a huge profit for himself. There were only two options available to me. I could sell cheap and lose a lot of money, or argue for the worth of my fur and force his hand. I decided to fight for a better price. At seventy dollars per marten, average, he would still make a handsome profit. Luckily Jen had taught me about the value of beaver castor. After the haggling over fur prices, I presented my stash of beaver castor. The buyer looked it over and payed top dollar. I think he saw me a bit differently after seeing I was not a pushover. Hopefully he would remember me and we could form a solid seller/buyer relationship over the upcoming years. We made over a thousand dollars on our dried castor glands. That was a nice bonus that I was not expecting.

When all was said and done, the dealer wrote me a check for twenty-two thousand two hundred and four dollars. We had hoped for a twenty-thousand-dollar payday. Needless to say, I was a happy man. With air under my feet, I trotted to the bank that was about ten blocks down the road, and after my business was completed there, made my way to check on my new snow machine. They had it ready, but I would not pick it up until a few hours before we were set to leave. The weather held nicely so we extended our stay for a couple more days. When it was time to leave, Jen's cousin, Andy, agreed to trailer the machine and haul it to the river so we would not damage the track or skis on the bare streets in Fairbanks. My business was done.

I walked in to Alice's house and found her and Jen at the table cutting potatoes for French fries. They were making supper and the menu included grilled chicken and baked beans, my favorite. The news from the doctor was excellent. Jen was in good health and the babies were growing as expected. I knew Jen wanted to have the babies at the cabin, so I was not surprised to hear her say, she had checked into the hiring of a midwife for five weeks. If we had the baby at Alice's home in Fairbanks, the cost would be five thousand dollars. If the midwife stayed at our cabin, the cost would be ten thousand dollars. She would cover her own transportation costs, as her husband was a pilot and had his own bush plane.

Jen said, "I know it is a lot of money, but I would really like to have the babies at home."

"I agree. Actually, I would want it no other way. That is our home and they should be born at home."

Alice joined the conversation and added, "You know, I could come out after the first two weeks and stay the month of June."

"Oh, Auntie, really!" Jen cried with delight. "That would be so sweet."

"Then let's do that," I said. "See if the midwife will agree to a two-week deal."

"I am sure she will," Jen said. Her schedule is full. Less time spent with us would be an advantage for her."

"Excellent! Make the deal."

"Do you have cash, Jen?" I asked.

"Yes, over two thousand dollars. I bring that stash with us on every trip."

"Do we pay upfront?"

One half up front to hold the dates, then the rest of the money is paid when her time with us is done."

"That will work great. I will have a lot of cash left over after I pay for the new machine, and then we will have enough at home to pay her if you pay the first half tomorrow."

"I will get everything lined up," Jen said.

It was good to have that taken care of. Now we could consider other things that needed our attention. We were out of rice and dried beans so the next day we hit the market. Our eating habits were changing and this meant less canned goods and more dried goods. From now on we would make our own baked beans from dried beans that we would purchase in bulk quantities. Rice, sugar, molasses, flour, salt, coffee, yeast, and spices pretty much completed our order. We did not need bacon or anything like that because of our stockpile of smoked meats. Eggs were essential and we bought an extra case because I was going to boil about fifty eggs, then slightly crack them and put them in the smokehouse. I read about this. They were supposed to be excellent. With some of them I wanted to go one step further and pickle them. That meant I had to add vinegar to my list.

Shopping with Jen was always fun. She seemed to have a rolling menu in her brain.

"Here," she said with excitement. "Noodles, we always forget about the noodles."

"Sweet, buy enough to last us through the summer."

Luckily, we could buy as much as we wanted of the pastas as each one was individually wrapped in one-pound packs, and then were encompassed in a bag of ten. Ten pounds of pasta. That should keep us for a while. We looked around the store for things we might find useful. It was then that we stumbled into the garden section that the store employees were just beginning to set up.

"We talked about a garden, Codi. Do you still want to do a garden?"

"Yes, I do."

"Should we buy some stuff here?"

"I don't know. I have not given it much thought."

Alice said, "We can order from a seed catalog online. That way you can investigate what will grow best this far north. Also, you can have them shipped to my house."

"That is good idea, Auntie."

"Okay," I said. "We will order seeds and have them flown out with the midwife in the middle of May. That will work out perfectly."

Before we left the garden section I bought a pack of tomato seeds and a pack each of bell peppers and broccoli seeds. I remembered a couple of times when my mom tried gardening. She loved broccoli and tomatoes and always started them inside the house.

Back at Alice's place we went online and ordered cucumbers, dill, radishes, turnips, carrots, cabbage, potatoes, beets, and squash seeds. I knew it was too much but we wanted to find out what would grow the best in our climate. We also wanted to figure out if certain vegetables would grow better with a little help from us. We heard a lot of people talk about makeshift greenhouses that would help out early in the year and also at the end of the year to extend the growing season. If this worked, we would be close to self-sufficient.

All visits have to end. The next morning, we hooked up with Andy and he picked up my machine and dropped me at the river. Jen met me there with her fully packed sled. We said our goodbyes knowing that we would see Alice in a couple months. It felt good to have everything taken care of as far as the babies were concerned.

## Chapter 23
## Back to the Cabin

The trip home was uneventful. The weather was warm, and if this kept up much longer, the river ice would disappear quickly under the ever-rising spring sun. We motored up and drove past the docked boat. I glanced over at it as if it were the first time I had noticed it. In fact, it was the first time I looked at it in months. The boat was tightly wrapped in tarps and seemed to have endured the winter winds quite well. The true story would be told after I got it unwrapped and back in the water. My biggest worry was that rodents had found a way in and done some damage by chewing on the seats or gnawing at the electrical wires.

Truth be told, I was ready for spring. The winter had been a hard one for both of us. We learned a lot over the past few months. However, more than anything else, our anticipation to be parents drove our desire for time to fly by. We were well stocked with essential items and ready for the babies to make their appearance. After the babies were born we would have to make a trip to Fairbanks by boat. We hoped that they would be a month old by then. Alice had a lot of experience with babies and children, and the midwife would help us greatly in those first two weeks.

After we go everything unpacked, I began work on my egg project. In a pot of boiling water, I added five dozen eggs and boiled them for two minutes and then let the eggs sit in the pot of hot water with the lid on for ten minutes. After the ten minutes was up, I spilled them out in the snow for a rapid cool down period. While they cooled in the snow bank outside the cabin door, I went to fire up the smokehouse. That is when I saw the last hind quarter of caribou meat. Without hesitation I sliced the rope that held it up and carried the semi-thawed meat into the cabin.

"I have to can this before the day is done." I said.

"You work on your project," Jen said. "I will take care of the meat."

"Thanks, Honey, I will help you after I get the smoker up and running."

"That sounds like a plan to me. See you in a little while."

There were enough racks in the smokehouse to hold all of the eggs, so after the smoke was rolling I gently made cracks in the eggs and placed them on racks. They would be fine on their own in the smoke house for a couple hours. Inside the cabin, I mixed up a brine for pickled eggs that I found in a recipe book which Alice had given us. If I did everything correctly, these eggs would last in their preserved state for several months. By the time I could help Jen, she had all the meat cut off the bones so I helped her chunk it up and pack in the jars. We kept one pile of the best cuts out so we could have one more meal of fresh, fried caribou for supper.

While we worked Jen and I discussed our plans for the upcoming year. First things first. Even though we had a huge supply of firewood, I wanted to spend at least one more day hauling wood from across the river, and so far, the ice was cooperating as the river had not begun to break up. Even though this was only my second year in the wilds of Alaska, I knew that there was no such thing as too much wood in the woodshed. My plan was simple. If there was nothing else to do, I would haul wood.

"At the rate you are going, we will be set for two winters," Jen said, during supper.

"I think you are right, and as long as I make some wood every year, we will always be one year ahead. Just the thought of having a stockpile of firewood is reassuring to me. After all, it is our most important chore."

Jen agreed, and then turned the conversation to the babies.

"Do you think we should take the children on the trap line next year or should I stay home with them?"

"I was thinking about that. On most days I figured I would run the lines, but it would be really cool if on nice days we could make it a family affair."

"That would be great, and is exactly what I think on the subject. We have to teach them early if we want them to really understand and treasure the life choice of living in the wild."

"Just think," I teased, "if we teach them right, in ten years we can send the kids out and you and I can stay here and bake cookies or something."

"Ha-ha, no! Not after what has happened the last two winters with Bill and Alvin and then you this year almost getting killed in the weather. No chance of that happening when they are that young."

"I agree, but do like the idea of trapping as a family."

"Me too. I grew up with my Auntie and Uncle always including me in everything they did. It was a spectacular life."

"Your life with them has given you a great deal of knowledge. I enjoy that about you. It makes you a great teacher to me. And, as I have proven, I need guidance once in a while."

"Ha-ha! Not funny. The bear attack and the storm incident from this year were learning tools. We never want to repeat those."

"Yes," I sincerely replied to Jen. "Those days are in the past."

We fell silent, as we often did during conversations. We were both reflective people, and spent a lot of time thinking about the past, the present, and the future of our lives."

I broke the silence.

"Tomorrow before I bring in the first load of wood, I want to scoot up the river and look for my rifle."

"That is a good idea. The weather is supposed to be beautiful."

"Do you want to go with me?"

"I do, but I better not. The ride from Fairbanks was pretty uncomfortable. My belly is getting hard to handle."

"Ha, but it is cute as all heck."

"Ha-ha, silly man, not to me."

"Okay, I will go out and look for my rifle. I sure hope that I come across it."

"You will."

The caribou was finally taken care of except for the pressure canning which Jen would finish up. After a great deal of hard work, all of our perishable foods were stored properly. I could not wait for the eggs to be done smoking. I went outside and turned the eggs over and figured that in a few more hours they would be ready to sample. While I was outside I gassed up my old snow machine and checked it over just to make sure it had held together. Other than it being ugly as all heck, everything looked to be in good working order. I continued to tool around outside doing little projects until my curiosity got the best of me. I decided to try one of the eggs. It was good, the smoke flavor just beginning to build. I wanted a stronger smoke flavor so left them in a bit longer to intensify the smoke flavor. While waiting for the smoking to be completed, I stacked firewood to fill the areas under the shed roof where we had depleted our supply during the winter. This gave me more room to pull up and drop off loads outside the shed and then to work at bucking it up whenever I had time.

Finally, the eggs were done. I rolled them into a big roaster pan that I used to transport smoked meats to the cabin. Inside, Jen and I worked for an hour taking the shells off the eggs. The brine was still warm and it smelled great. I poured it over the eggs once they were packed in two, one-gallon plastic jars that we had saved. A thick layer of onions covered the top. Down in the subterranean refrigerator they went. It would be a couple weeks before they would be fully pickled and we could taste them.

The days were just about twelve hours long now. We could still see across the river at seven in the evening. More impressively, it was light at about seven thirty in the morning. This was good for many reasons. There was always work to do and I usually found myself working on the woodpile or preparing the traps for next year. Those were always the two major jobs that absolutely had to be done. The cabin had withstood the winter assault and looked good from all angles. Jen spent most of her time in the cabin. She was setting up everything that would help us take care of the babies. They would sleep upstairs with us. I was happy that we decided to leave the upstairs one big room. The cribs were on one side of the bed, along with a table and comfortable chair that Jen purchased in Fairbanks. We were set. Come on babies.

I was up early the next morning. Besides recovering my rifle and dragging some logs back, I wanted to explore some trapping and hunting land across the river. To make sure I had everything needed for the day, I did a quick inventory. Gas, oil, chainsaw, and tools—they were all there. After a quick trip into the cabin to say goodbye to Jen, I was off and across the river. I decided to make a big loop out and around, with my final destination being the spot where my rifle was waiting in the snow. With the temperatures as warm as they were, the snow would begin melting fast in the next few days. We had lost some to this point, but because the temps usually reached the freezing mark at night, the melt had been slow. Besides that, potentially, there was a lot of winter type weather that could surprise us.

My journey was exciting. There were plenty of new spots to trap and to hunt. On one hillside about ten miles from our home, I stumbled upon a small cabin. It was about twelve feet by twelve feet and built out of peeled spruce logs. The roof was sod and the structure seemed fairly sound. There were no windows in it and the door needed considerable work as did the walls. In several places the chink material had fallen out leaving long gaps between the logs that if not fixed would allow the cold winter air to pass through. This could easily be fixed. There was a small stove in one corner with a stove pipe attached that went up and then through the wall. On the outside it extended to just above the roof line. Overall, the cabin looked like it could be of use to me.

After looking the place over, I knew it would serve us as a trapping outpost cabin for me. In other words, we could extend our trap line further out and use this as a sleepover spot. It would save us a lot of travel time. All we needed to do to make it comfortable was to fix the walls, the door, and then add a couple of cots and our sleeping gear. Of course, we would have to bring food and water, and if we stocked the place with some pots and pans, we would be set. I was excited to tell Jen about my find.

Because of the little cabin's location my exploration could progress further out and away from the river. Everywhere I went seemed to be untouched by humans. I saw no sign that any trapper had visited the area for a long time. As I continued on my trip, something caught my attention down in a long, sloping valley. At first, I could not identify what I was looking at. As I closed the distance, I recognized a huge moose rack partially buried in the snow. It had been there for years, and after digging it from the snow, noticed that it was untouched by rodents. This was a sweet find and would look great hanging on the front of the woodshed. I threw it on the sled and tied it down. I motored the machine to the top of the hill and scanned the area. More of the same terrain lay before me. If everything worked out as planned in my mind, this coming winter would offer us some great trapping and hunting. Our future in the wild looked brighter than ever. Coming across that little cabin was a stroke of good luck. Luck was a welcome ingredient to well-made plans.

I had seen enough for now, so I turned the machine back toward the river. When I reached the spot where I rolled my snow machine everything seemed surreal, almost like I had never been there. The wind and melting snow had changed the entire scene. At the edge of the embankment is where I found my rifle. It was undamaged. As I looked over the steep bank I could not figure out how it was that my rifle was at the top of the bank undamaged, rather than somewhere down the slope cracked up and in pieces. My only thought was that it must have come off of my shoulder at the beginning of my tumble. *Oh well*, I thought, *at least I found it*. All that needed doing was a good cleaning job and to get it sighted in before the next use.

The bank was too steep to drive down, so I motored downstream until the slope was less intimidating and drove onto the river. The ice seemed good, but about halfway across, I hit overflow. I punched the throttle but still sunk about a foot. Slush and water were flying up and over the sled but my pace never slowed. I did not let off the gas until I reached the shore on the other side. My thoughts immediately went to Alvin and Bill. Overflow is what killed them. Their situation was much worse than this, but a person never knows how bad overflow will be until he hits it.

Because of the warming temperatures and the incident with the overflow, I decided not to cross the river anymore until next winter. There was plenty of wood for me to pick up on this side of the river. As I headed for home, I kept my eye out for suitable firewood, and whenever I came across an area with a growth of standing dead spruce, I cut them down and loaded as many of the logs on the sled as I could pull. There was so much that I could not carry it all, so I left them lay, and over the course of the spring would make several trips back and forth to pick up all the wood.

## Chapter 24
### Names for our Children

Time flew by until we got to April. All of our work was done except for the daily needs of keeping the cabin operational. We could not go anywhere on snow machines because the river ice was gone in some spots and breaking up in all the other areas. The weather had remained relatively mild throughout the spring and all of the snow was gone by the third week of April.

One evening Jen and I were sitting outside enjoying a late-night campfire. It was ten o'clock and the sun was still shining high in the sky. We began to talk about baby names. As we talked it became clear that we wanted Bill and Alvin's names to be included somehow in the names of our children.

"I have always liked the name, Zenia," remarked Jen.

"I like that for a girl, but what about a middle name for a girl?"

"I hope you are not thinking Bill or William or Alvin."

"Ha-ha, no." Just then the name Alvie popped in my head. Hey, what about Alvie?"

"Zenia Alvie? I like that."

"Me too. If we have one girl, her name will be Zenia Alvie?" I asked.

"Yes," Jen said. "I like that a lot."

"What if we have two girls?"

"Hmmm," I considered. That is a tough one. Let's hope for a boy and a girl."

"Okay, what about boy's names?"

"I don't know. Do you want Codi William?"

"No. I like William, but really like the name Emerson."

"Emerson William?"

"Yes."

"I like it, Jen said. "I like it a great deal."

"Good. Me too. Emerson William it is."

"Sweet. That was easy."

"Now, Jen, make sure you don't mess up our plans by having two boys or two girls."

She giggled sweetly and grabbed my hand. "You silly man, I can't control that."

I pulled her close and we sat for a long time without talking. This life was so good for the both of us and our children. We knew that they would flourish here.

The river had cleared up nicely. We were done with week one of May, and Jen figured the babies might come earlier than originally thought. We hoped the midwife would arrive sooner than the due date.

I had already started my tomato and broccoli plants and they were doing well. They were facing the sun in the south windows of our bedroom. The plants were about three inches tall and looked very healthy. As the days ticked by, Jen stayed inside more often and I continued to ramble about and do things outside. The river was not only clear of ice but had receded to near normal level. That was interesting because we had received a great deal of snow, but then I remembered that it melted at a slower pace and over a longer period of time, which kept it from rising above flood stage.

I wandered down to the river with the full intention of putting the dock system and boat in the river. When I reached the boat, I was startled to see a bear walking up the bank partially obscured by the boat and dock. I stopped and made no movement as the bear continued toward me. *No gun*, I thought. *Nice move.*

The bear stopped suddenly and raised its nose high in the air and sniffed noisily. The bear's actions looked familiar to me, and I sensed it was my bear. After a few seconds of no movement from either of us, I worked up the nerve and whispered,

"Pretty Girl, is that you?"

All I could hear were snorts and air being sucked in through nostrils. My heart was pounding. I could only hope it was her. The bear was skinny, but its body frame was much larger than Pretty Girl's compared to the last time I had seen her. There was not much to do, yet something had to be done. I back stepped toward the cabin, my head never turning to look where I was going. The bear noticed me, and took a few steps forward. It was Pretty Girl. She had a cute little notch on her left ear and once she got past the boat I recognized it. I kept my eyes on her and kept walking backwards. Once at the cabin, I opened the door and stood there waiting for my little bear to come up. She took her time. About halfway to the cabin I noticed some scurrying behind her. She had cubs, two of them.

My heart soared. "Jen?" I whisper shouted. "It's Pretty Girl, and she has babies!"

"Seriously?"

"Yes, she is on the path leading up from the river. Come see them."

Jen came over just as the three bears got to the woodshed. Pretty Girl was very cautious. She knew us well, but had to mind her natural senses in order to care for her cubs. She walked toward the cabin and then thought better of it and retreated to the side of the shed. She seemed to know that she belonged here. It is hard to know what a wild animal is actually feeling, but in her mind, I am sure she knew she was safe.

The little cubs scurried about her and were as cute as anything a person could imagine.

"Oh," Jen said, "They are so darn cute."

"I know. They are so tiny, like a furry basketball."

"Ha, that's funny."

"I hope they stay close by. Maybe she will use the den I dug for her as a summer sleeping spot."

"That would be neat, but I bet she ventures off and becomes completely wild before the summer is done."

"I guess. It is so nice to see her. I thought that when we saw her kill that caribou, it was the end of our relationship."

"I wonder where her den is," Jen said.

"I would like to know that too."

"Sometime when she wanders off, I will follow her and see where she goes."

"Her presence brings up a potential problem. The midwife will be here in a couple days. We have to keep an ear out for the plane so we can warn them of her presence."

"Yes," I said. "I will pay close attention to that."

After about an hour of me sitting and watching the cubs nurse, Pretty Girl got up and wandered up the hill by her den, sniffed around for a minute or two, and then walked away. That was the last time I saw her all summer.

Because my nerves were a bit frazzled in anticipation for the baby's arrival, and Jen having several episodes when she thought the baby was coming out, I started hoeing the garden plot. It amazed me how much work a guy can get done when his mind never ventures from one thought. The babies were on the way and that meant added responsibility for me. Creating a garden that would produce healthy food and eventually have my children working in it, drove my work attitude.

I finally looked up and surveyed what I had accomplished. There was a lot of torn up area, enough to plant everything we desired to put in the ground. I wanted to put some plants in the ground to see how they would do this early in the year. Because I had one hundred or so broccoli plants, I decided to take twenty of them and put them out as the first garden test of my life. The soil was quite warm and the plants seemed to like their new freedom for growth. Time would tell the story.

## Chapter 25
## Time for the Babies

After I gathered up the garden tools and started for the shed, I heard the unmistakable sound of an airplane. On the horizon above the river bed came a small plane with floats for landing gears. Within a minute, the pilot reduced his power and glided the plane to a perfect landing on the water. He guided the plane toward the shore and then killed the engines. As he neared the shoreline and realized he had enough propulsion to reach shore, he stepped out on the float and said, "I am Steve. I am delivering your midwife, Deanna."

"Hi Steve, I am Codi."

"Hello Codi, no baby yet, I hope."

"No, not yet. Soon however."

He threw me a rope and I grabbed it and pulled the floats onto the sand just enough so they would hold the plane steady after it was tied off to a log. The passenger door opened, and out popped Deanna. "Hi Codi, your wife has told me a lot about you."

"All good, I hope."

"Yes, all good."

"How is Jen feeling?"

"Like a couple babies are on the way." I said.

"Good, I finished another delivery earlier than expected, so after a day to rest, I figured it best that I get out here."

"Excellent. I am happy you are here, and Jen will be ecstatic. She is nervous about giving birth."

"That is to be expected, especially the first go around."

"Here, let me help you with those bags."

I took one suitcase from Steve and one from Deana. "Is this everything?"

"Not quite," responded Steve, "but I can handle the rest."

"Okay, we will head to the cabin, just follow the trail, and, oh yeah, we do have a bear with cubs in the area."

"Oh, what a thrill," Steve said shakily. "Wait for me."

"Okay."

We walked the distance to the cabin and as we did, I told them about Pretty Girl and her cubs. They were impressed with the story. When we arrived in the cabin, Jen was standing by the stove with an impatient look on her face.

"Hi Deanna," She said weakly.

"Hi Jen. Do you feel alright?"

"Yes, just very tired."

"Okay, let's get you up to bed and I will see how close we are to the big moment."

"Hopefully, we are there." Jen replied.

"By the way, this is my husband, Steve. You did not get to meet him when we set up this appointment."

"Hi Steve."

The two women disappeared up the stairs. I showed Steve around the place until he thought it was time for him to fly out. We went back inside where he said goodbye to Deanna and gave her a satellite phone to use for emergencies. It was a big contraption but would enable Deanna to call to Fairbanks if we needed any kind of help. Steve would be ready to fly out and deliver something or pick her up. Just before he left, Steve reminded me that the seeds we ordered were still on the plane. We walked down to the river to get the package. We talked for a short while about our lives out in the wild and their lives in the city. He was an interesting guy. When Steve was ready, I gave him a shove away from the shoreline. He started the engine and coasted out to the middle of the river and faced upstream. He waved from the cockpit window, revved up the engine and took to the air. Within minutes he was gone from my sight.

I was excited to look over the seed selection, and then get some of the cool weather seeds planted. First, I went inside to see if there was anything for me to do. Jen was sleeping. Deanna told me that she was only hours away from giving birth and that everything looked good for an uncomplicated birth. I told her that I would be outside and to holler if she needed anything.

After sorting the seeds, it was clear to me that the radishes, onions, cabbage, and potatoes would be the place to start. I spent the rest of the afternoon planting seeds and marking the rows so I did not trample already planted areas. When that was done, I went inside to cook supper. I made a casserole out of canned pike, noodles, cream of mushroom soup, and canned peas. It was delicious. Jen got up and came downstairs but could not tolerate the thought of eating anything. Deanna and I ate and then we sat and talked for a bit. Jen wanted to go back to bed. We helped her up the stairs and then I went to water the items I had planted. To pass the time and to expel pent up energy and anxiousness, I hauled five-gallon buckets of water, two at a time from the river.

It was dark by the time all of my work was done. I went inside and then upstairs. Jen was in labor.

"Sit down beside her, Codi. She has just gone into labor."

"Okay."

I did as I was told. Jen immediately grabbed my hand and held on tight.

"Are you okay, honey?"

"Yes," she said between breaths, "but it hurts."

"What can I do?"

"Just be here with me, hold my hand."

"Okay, I won't leave you."

"Thanks," she groaned.

Another labor pain hit. I could see by Jen's contorted face that it was a big one. When it was done, Deanna said it was more intense than the last few and that we needed to prepare for the babies coming very soon. Everything blurred for me after that. I saw it all happen in real time, but it seemed like slow motion for most of the birth. When it was all said and done, I came back to reality and saw Jen holding our two lovely babies. On her left arm was our beautiful Emerson William and on her right arm was the beautiful Zenia Alvie. Jen was smiling broadly. Everything seems intensely quiet. It was a wonderful scene to behold.

"I am a father."

"Yes, you are, silly man."

"And you are a mother."

"Yes. Isn't it lovely?"

"That it is, for sure."

"Can I hold one or both?"

"Yes," said Deanna. "Sit in that chair and I will bring them to you."

I sat down but my nerves jingled and jangled as Deanna handed me the first tiny bundle. It was Zenia. She was so tiny.

"Hi, my little trapper." It was all I could think to say. I lifted her to my face and kissed my child. What a beautiful experience. After Emerson was laid in the crook of my other arm, I repeated the same affection. They were wonderful little babies.

Jen lay in bed exhausted. Her smile, however, was beaming wide.

"You are a daddy. What do you think about that?"

"I love it." How do we feed them?"

"You let me worry about that. You can do all the diaper changes. That should be a fair trade."

"What, diapers?"

"Yes, silly man. Babies poop."

"Oh yeah, I guess they do. All the diapers, I have to change all of them?"

"No! Just teasing you. Most of that work will be mine."

The wonder of the moment took over as we held the babies for a long time, simply admiring their beauty. After a while, Jen drifted in and out of sleep and finally fell into a deep sleep. The babies slept soundly for about an hour. They had eaten right after birth, but, judging by their cries after waking up, they were hungry again. Deanna came and took Zenia to Jen while I sat with Emerson. When she was done eating, I burped my daughter while my son got a belly full. After the kids were fed, Jen went straight back to sleep. She deserved the rest.

Our nights were not quiet and peaceful any more. The babies slept quite well, but there was always one feeding about midnight and one about four in the morning. That was not too bad according to Deanna. The two weeks with the midwife went by quickly and on the morning of her fourteenth day, we heard the plane come in for a landing. Aunt Alice was on board and would stay with us for the month of June. After she got settled in and a few days went by, I began work on the garden. The potatoes were popping up through the ground.

Things were going perfectly well for us. I spent a lot of time with the babies and found it so neat to see their personalities begin to develop. It was also nice that Aunt Alice could be there to help Jen and to get to know her great-niece and great-nephew.

In my spare time, I planted more garden items and everything seemed to be doing quite well. If the crops turned out as good as expected, we would have to make a boat trip to Fairbanks to get more jars and other canning supplies.

On many days Jen and Aunt Alice would join me in the garden. Jen was very excited about our new-found venture and excited for the preserving of all of this great food. As the month passed we began harvesting from the garden. The early crops of onions and radishes were growing quickly and were more than welcome on our dinner table. The long daylight hours really help, and to add to that, the weather was exceptional. We received enough rain to keep the ground moist and enough warm sunshine to keep the soil warm. That summer was the perfect growing season.

It finally came time when Aunt Alice had to leave. We did not like to see her go. She was such a great help, but more than that, we loved to have her in our home. Before she left, we told her that we would be in town in a few weeks to buy the needed items for canning our vegetables. The good thing was that after paying Deanna, we still had a few thousand dollars remaining from our money earned by trapping. Once we bought all of the needed items and restocked our fuel barrels, we would likely be out of money. That was okay. With high expectations for the upcoming trapping season, we might double the amount we had made. If that happened, we would have no reason to spend any of the money we had in the bank.

July came in with a bang. The wind and rain were relentless for the first few days of the month. Most of the garden plants made it through the weather onslaught, with the biggest casualty being the corn stalks. After the weather settled down, I went out to the garden and braced up all the damaged plants by packing soil around the base of their stems. This seemed to work well, and after all was done, not much permanent damage had been inflicted. As I looked around I could see that we would have cabbages that would be bigger than a basketball. The broccoli plants were beginning to form heads and everything else looked well. I picked a medium sized cabbage and took it with me back to the cabin.

"Hey Jen, check this out," I said as I burst through the door.

I startled her and the babies. They both began to cry as Jen shot me a dirty look.

"Codi, they just fell asleep."

"Oops, sorry. I was excited to show you this cabbage."

I went to the place they were lying on the floor and laid down next to the babies and stroked their heads and talked softly to them. They went back to sleep in a few minutes.

"Thanks," Jen said. "I needed a break."

I lifted myself up from the floor and went over and gave Jen a big hug. I saw some tears slowly running down her cheeks.

"What's the matter, Honey?"

"Oh, nothing really. I think I am super-tired. I feel like I could sleep for a week. Breast feeding the children takes a lot of time and energy. I really never get a good night's sleep."

How can we fix this?" I asked.

"Well, I think we should take a trip to Fairbanks to get all of our supplies and for the kids to get checkups. I will ask the doctor if it is okay to breastfeed and use a milk formula interchangeably. If we can do that, the babies would eventually be weaned off of breast milk."

"That sounds like a great plan."

"It does, and the best thing of all is that then you can feed the babies while I sleep."

"Awesome, I am happy to do that. When do you want to leave?"

"We can go anytime."

"Okay," I said. "For the rest of the day, I will do some maintenance on the boat and fill the tank with gas. After that I will be set to go first thing tomorrow morning."

"Great. I will get things packed and be ready."

Before going outside to work on the boat, I sat down, and with Jen's help, made a list of everything we needed to do while in town. Then, because we decided to build shelves to store all of our canned goods, I measured the wall in the addition that was farthest from the stove. Because I

wanted the shelves to look neat, I planned to buy
enough lumber to build doors to hide the shelves.
When they were all done, I pictured them as floor to
ceiling cupboards. I knew Jen would be happy with
my plan.

# Chapter 26
## Baby Trappers get a Checkup

Early the next morning, the four of us left the cabin for Fairbanks. It was a pleasant morning, and judging by the weather at that time, it would be a great day to be on the water. We took our time on the way down river. Zenia and Emmerson were enjoying the sunshine and seemed to be mesmerized by the hum of the motor and the general movements of the boat as it glided on top of the glass-smooth surface. They both went to sleep after about twenty minutes into the journey. Jen sat close to them on the bench seat that ran the length of the right side of the boat. With one hand on each child, she dozed off to sleep too. The three of them looked comfortable. I hoped Jen would get enough sleep to energize her for the day. To help her out, I slowed the boat down to the point where we were going about one third of the speed we had been cruising at. It was a good pace, and would give Jen about an extra hour of sleep. I really hoped the babies could go on formula. If so, I would take over many of the feedings so Jen could recuperate faster. Carrying two babies for nine months and then caring for their every need after that, was an intensive time for any mother.

Luck was with us, Jen did not stir until I pulled back on the throttle slowing the boat down to a crawl as we approached the landing outside of

Fairbanks. I gently bumped the bow up to the river's edge, then jumped out and tied the boat to a nearby dock post. While the babies slept and Jen sat with them, I trotted to a nearby store to call Aunt Alice and ask her if she would pick us up. Of course, she was more than pleased to do so. Only minutes after I reached the boat, Alice was there. Our greeting hugs were as special as always, but her eyes never left the babies. As Jen laid one child in each of her arms, I could hear little, loving coos coming from Aunt Alice. The sound made me think of mourning doves. Her interaction with the babies was special to witness. She was a special woman. I realized at that time how lucky I was to have her in my life. We headed straight back to Alice's house so Jen could feed the now energized babies who were growing slowly irritable because the dinner plate was not before them. The babies were tuckered out and went to sleep as soon as they finished eating. We had quiet time and could visit with Alice. The babies slept for several hours, so during that time Jen called the doctor to make an appointment and to ask if the babies could go on formula. The nurse she talked to said she did not anticipate a problem, but would rather the doctor make that decision after seeing the babies. We had no problem with that because the appointment was for the following morning.

Jen wanted to take a nap. Alice said she would watch over the children while I ran errands to buy most of what we needed to take back with us. After all of the shopping was done I loaded the lumber and the jars in the boat where it was docked. That worked out great because most of my work was done. Also, over the last year, we made friends with an old man who lived next to the boat ramp. He allowed us to tie up on his dock and promised to keep an eye on our boat and materials.

After a week in Fairbanks we knew it was time to get back home. We said our goodbyes and started our journey back to the cabin early on a Monday morning. There was so much that had to be done before winter. The upcoming winter would be my third out here in the wilderness. In some ways it felt like I was always here, like the first eighteen years of my life were nonexistent. It was a strange feeling. Both Jen and I loved this life and would trade it for nothing in this world. Our children were doing well and growing every day.

The rest of July and all of August were spent canning vegetables and picking and canning blueberries. When we were in Fairbanks, I had bought an additional two hundred and fifty canning jars. We were well on our way to filling them. It was a good feeling to see our first garden produce so much food. We hoped it was not simply beginners' luck, because we did not know much about gardening, and we were adamant about preserving as much as possible.

Early in September I finished building the shelves that would store all of our goods. Because the shelves were deep enough for three-quart jars to fit, and had doors on them, it took up some of the living space in the addition. The trade off, we decided, was well worth the loss of livable space.

The next project that needed to be completed was the fix up work on the old cabin that I had found across the river. It would be essential to our trapping success the following year. To make the job easier, we needed to get the four-wheeler across the river so I built a platform in the back of the boat that was big enough for the wheeler to sit on. Once that was completed, I built a ramp on the river edge that would allow me to drive the wheeler up and onto the ramp. I had seen this down in Fairbanks and it looked like a great way to haul machines around.

After all tools were rounded up, Jen decided that she and the children would like to join me on the trip out to the old cabin. We would spend several days there, so she lined up all the things we would need. She found pots and pans that could be used out there. I loaded all of the kitchen stuff onto the boat. Most of it fit under the platform I built. We also had three cots that were purchased for the purpose of being used out there. A supply of canned goods were the last things I put in the boat. We left the following morning. When we got across the river, I unloaded everything from the boat and then took Jen and the kids to the cabin so they could start setting things up while I returned for the remaining supplies. There was not much seating room left on the four-wheeler after I got everything strapped to the racks, but Jen settled in and when she was ready, I placed a baby in each of her arms. We were ready.

The cabin looked the same as it did in the winter. There was still no sign that anyone had visited the place since I had been there. Once Jen and the kids were settled in and we had a couple of the cots opened up, I returned for another load of supplies. It made me nervous to leave my family, even if it was only for an hour or so. Jen did have her rifle and one of my pistols. She knew how to use them, and would definitely put them into action if needed. Still, the worry persisted. I hoped it was only the worries of a new and inexperienced father. I hoped.

Printed in Great Britain
by Amazon

84325742R10140